Wild Words
Volume 7

Wild Words Children's Book Festival,
c/o The Reading Room,
Bridge Street,
Carrick on Shannon,
Co. Leitrim,
Ireland.

+353 (71) 96 71580

www.wildwords.ie

Published by Leitrim County Council Arts Office.

www.leitrimarts.ie

ISBN: 978-0-9576189-9-2

Edited by Helen Carr.

A collection of writing by young people produced as part of the
Wild Words Children's Book Festival, Carrick on Shannon, Co. Leitrim.

Introduction

By Helen Carr

This is the seventh volume of the annual Wild Words collection of writing by young people aged between fourteen and eighteen. I've been involved with the judging, selecting and editing of the book since the very beginning, and it never ceases to amaze me how it's grown and blossomed from year to year. It seems like every year there are more entries, from a greater number of counties in Ireland, in an ever-evolving array of genres and writing styles – poetry, blank verse, first and third person narrative, essays and poems on everything from very modern themes to magic realism, science fiction and historical fiction. I've come to think of the early summer as 'Wild Words season' and always look forward to seeing what kind of work the perspectives and preoccupations of this new crop of young and emerging writers will provoke.

Something I always love about the writing in Wild Words is its immediacy and passion. For writers in their teens, many experiences and feelings are new, or more vividly felt than at any other time in life, and the strength of those emotions, convictions and concerns comes across so powerfully in the works in this volume; universal literary themes like love, loss, coming of age, fear, courage and prejudice are made new and fresh through the words of these young writers.

I really noticed the increase in the amount of poetry submitted in 2018's Wild Words competition, and that has continued this year, with more poetry than ever before both submitted and selected. Perhaps award-winning YA-writer and poet Sarah Crossan's tenure as Laureate na nÓg and the work of performance poets like Colm Keegan has freed poetry from the classroom and given it back to young writers as a valuable and flexible means of expression? Writers often reflect on the world around them, and as well as issues that may be more specific to young writers – nostalgia for childhood, concerns about navigating the world of teenage tribes and social media, sport and competition – this year there were noticeably more works on environmental themes submitted. This chimes with the urgent realisation of the dangers of climate change and pollution and the urgent need for a more sustainable way of life, which was expressed by young people around the world this year at the School Strikes for Climate, when 1.4 million students participated in rallies urging adults to take responsibility and stop climate change.

One of the primary goals of writing is to communicate – the writer is reaching out to express something to their readers, who in turn, make it their own as they read it and identify with characters or themes. While judging the submissions, I was looking for compelling storylines, well-handled plots, strong, convincing characters and the ability to express feelings in words. I think all the pieces in this collection display these traits, but above all, as a reader, I felt really drawn in to all the chosen works; reading them is like a conversation between writer and reader.

Selecting the forty-eight pieces published in Wild Words Volume 7 from the more than 260 submitted was no easy task, but reading the submissions was a pleasure and assured me that writing, imagination and facility of expression are still very strong in Ireland, and our literary tradition is in safe hands going into the future. Stephen King – a writer who knows how to tell a story, and a lifelong reader – expressed the power of the printed word when he said, 'Books are a uniquely portable magic.' Wild Words Volume 7 is packed with forty-eight unique brands of magic. Read, be transported and enjoy!

Helen Carr

June 2019

Helen Carr has worked in publishing for over twenty years and is Senior Editor with The O'Brien Press. She has worked with many Irish children's and YA authors, including Judi Curtin, Sarah Webb, Kim Hood, Alan Nolan, Erika McGann, Ger Siggins, Ruth Frances Long, Chris Judge, Nicola Colton and Sarah Bowie. Helen has also reviewed books for many publications, including The Sunday Independent, Inis magazine and BookFest and regularly speaks at publishing events and on panels.

Contents

A Day at the Beach

By Caolan Roberts, age 14.

I remember the seagulls screeching above me.
Their glossy white feathers
Stark against the gun-metal grey clouds,
Smothering the sky.

I remember the sharp sea wind,
Sending daggers of sea spray towards me;
They lashed my face with their stinging blades.

I remember the charging cavalry of waves,
Rampaging towards my brother and me.
Their white-crested manes blowing in the wind,
As we tried to leap over them like Olympic athletes
Gliding over hurdles.

I recall the gloopy golden sand sucking,
My then-tiny toes and
The gritty grains stuck under my nails,
As my brother and I made
Grand Sandcastles,
Like eccentric architects.
With moats as deep as the incoming sea,
Spires that reached the ominous clouds.

RUN, BOY, RUN.

By Aaliyah Mullen, age 14.

Boy had been running since he could remember. He hadn't a name, hadn't a family, hadn't a home. Just him, his fifteen years, and his feet versus the hunt. This is why, as he woke up in the damp hollow just underneath a bridge, he quickly rose to action. His back ached, his throat burned and his hunger pains had worsened overnight. He ignored them. He took a quick perimeter check, his trusty club in hand, searching for a sign of his predators. A stone out of place, a dropped bullet casing, anything. He found nothing. Relief surged through him. The sun had just begun to rise. Orange and yellow light trickled through the cracks of the bridge. From what he could tell, like most things since The End twenty years ago, this bridge had been long abandoned and surrendered to nature. He returned to the hollow and rifled through his bag, pouring its limited contents over the floor. A worn jacket tumbled to the ground, followed by a nutrition bar. Nothing else.

With a frustrated scream, Boy threw his bag against the wall. He couldn't afford another supply run. They were catching up with him. Forget about surviving the next year. At this rate, he only had a couple of days left. Panic welled up inside his stomach. He collapsed against the wall, fear clouding his thoughts. His fingers curled in his hair, pulling. His arms trembled.

He hated this sick 'game'. Could it even be called that? What sort of twisted world hunted a child for sport? Because he could do things they couldn't? Bad excuse. He couldn't dwell on it. He needed to think. He could do that.

He thought he saw an old supermarket a few kilometres back. But he couldn't turn back. That put less distance between him and them. Sometimes Boy thought of them as wolves. Snarling, growling beasts ready to gobble him up if he made the slightest mistake.

The thought of continuing onward made his blood run cold. There was a small town approximately ten kilometres from here. He could justify a pause if it was a quick. With him needing everything he could get his hands on, he was looking at two days.

Boy had never remained in a place for more than two days since he was eight. He'd had a close encounter with a group of his hunters and had barely escaped with his life and reminders – large scars on his leg and torso and an ugly slash across his chin. He'd been lucky that the hunters hadn't a good grasp with their knives or enough bullets to catch him. Boy shouldn't -- wouldn't – risk it. But he had to.

His hands let go of his hair and he uncurled himself. He took a deep breath, tucked his club into his belt and grabbed his bag. Snatching up the nutrition bar and taking a large bite, he clamoured his way out of the hollow.

Standing in broad daylight was the riskiest time for Boy. Anyone could see him. Anyone could take a shot at him and he'd be none the wiser. He quickly broke into a sprint. He felt the wind hit his face. Ash blew into his eyes from the ruined terrain. Nevertheless, he continued.

As it turned out, the town was closer than he thought. It had taken him an hour to get there. Boy wiped his eyes in his sleeve and grimaced as a chalky brown substance appeared on the cloth. He began to survey the town from a distance. He clutched his club tightly. An old habit. A useful habit. He ducked behind a boulder. A beaten army tank rode into town, two blonde heads poking out, guns trained on the terrain. Most likely looking for him- Or rather, the sum he would bring if they caught him.

Let them, he thought angrily. As if it'd be that easy.

A few of the townspeople, mouths wrapped in cloth for protection, trailed the outskirts, looking for things to scavenge. Town mustn't see a lot of new people. Good. That'd work in his favour. Nothing else came in the hours that then passed. No threats, other than the tank, which would be easily avoidable. It wasn't as if he'd be looking for trouble anyway. He could do it.

The sky began to darken. He hoped that it wasn't rain. Rain was horrible. Rain meant that he could get sick. Sick meant slow. That's how the others before him got caught. Poor prey made docile by illness or injury and caught by their predators. That was the one thing Boy would refuse to happen. If he had to die, he'd die on his feet, club in hand, fighting until he couldn't any more.

The horizon turned red and shadows stretched across the ruined landscape. Boy waited until the sunset had faded and black took its place. Under the cover of night, he moved to begin his reconnaissance inside.

Town was small. Half of the buildings were in ruins, and presumably wouldn't contain anything of use to him. The others mostly seemed occupied by the townspeople. The tank had been left running. Boy heard the engine softly whirl from where it was parked outside a large warehouse. He bit back a scoff. Cocky decision. There wasn't much fuel around these days. They were expecting someone. Expecting him? The question was if they know he needed supplies and expecting him, or trying their luck. Probably the latter; he doubted their intelligence. Boy pressed a fingertip to the tank, watching with mild amusement as the engine slowly chugged to a stop. No modifications against him made. A smile curled on Boy's face. How arrogant. He was used to being hunted. It wasn't often he got to tip the scales, even in small ways. But first he needed to finish what he came to do. Find supplies.

A makeshift farm had been set up behind a crumbling shack. Fresh produce wasn't much use to Boy. It went off easily and was barely edible. Soil had been ruined during The End and nothing had grown very well since. That left Boy with only one other option.

An old ruined general store sat hidden behind some collapsing huts. It looked to still contain food and clothes. Bingo. Boy pressed his face lightly to the dusty, dirty glass and peered in. The clothes looked to be in decent condition. Muted colours and made of materials that would last him a good while. His eyes quickly darted around the store, picking out which items he needed. His shirt had a large gash in the back- he needed a new one. His current trousers trailed his shins. And shoes; those heavy boots in the corner would last him a year. He moved onto food. A box of nutrition bars he could nab, some tinned foods, rice! He found rice once before and he had enjoyed it. He'd take that too.

There was a loud curse somewhere behind him. Boy jumped and dived behind the ruins of a building for cover. In the darkness he could make out blonde hair. One of the blondes was bent over the tank, cursing, hitting and kicking the engine. Boy hid a grin. It wouldn't be working for a while.

Boy didn't have a good grasp on his abilities yet. He didn't know his limits, his strengths, the hows or whys. Here's what he did know: He was able to manipulate engines. He had abilities. And that the entire society that had been built after the apocalypse – more commonly referred to as 'The End' – wanted to kill him for it.

Boy watched as the other blonde stumbled out of the warehouse, rubbing sleep from her eyes and hissing at her co-rider. He couldn't make out what he was saying. Boy quickly tried to decide his plan of action. He had wanted to try the stores door, check the lock and see if he could pick it. If not, he would have smashed the window and grabbed whatever he could before making a break for it. He couldn't risk it when both blondes were roaming the streets. He didn't think they'd be smart enough to seek him out but if they saw him in their turf, Boy might as well have painted a target on his chest in neon letters. He'd need to leave it for tonight. He'd try again tomorrow night. He'd rather not be stuck in the one place for another day. Unfortunately, he would be.

The blondes began arguing, beginning in low voices before rising in volume until they were shouting. Boy took the opportunity to slip away. He'd seen a cave about a kilometre away. That'd be good for tonight. Every step he took felt as if he was sinking into the ground, matching the feeling of his stomach sinking in a dread he couldn't place. He collapsed into the cave, adrenaline fading and exhausting taking over. In the cold cave, Boy felt worse than he had all day. He fell into uneasy sleep.

Boy dreamed in fear. He was six years old again and barely surviving. His feet dragged on the barren ground; eyes painfully dry from the heat. He was tired, he was starving, he was thirsty and all he wanted was for people to stop shooting at him. How long had he been walking? All he could see was ruin. Somewhere, he heard the click of a barrel. He started to run and a stray bullet grazed his shoulder. Boy held back a sob.

Underneath his feet, the world shifted. His shoulder was still bleeding, He's still six and the blondes are stood in front of him, guns trailed at his nose. His heart shot to his throat. No, no, no, no.

'End of the line, kid,' said the woman.

'No hard feelings, yeah? It's just business.' said the man.

Boy wanted to shout and scream, anger and fear pumping through his veins. This wasn't fair. It wasn't fair. A thousand words flew through his head, like bats screeching at intruders. His hand itched for his club. But he couldn't move.

'No.' He whispered. He hadn't spoken in months. His voice was dry and croaky and every word hurt. The man grinned maliciously, raising a hand to his ear. Repeat yourself, he dared. Curses gathered in Boy's mind. He felt sick. He refused to be entertainment, pressing his lips tightly together. No. If he were to die with no way out, he'd do it with his pride. Even if he hadn't much left.

'Well?' asked the man. Boy glared. The woman whistled a short tune, mouth twisted into a sadistic smirk. The man's face lost his. The next thing Boy knew, pain shot through the side of his face and he fell to the ground. He attempted to stumble back to his feet (die with two feet on the ground, standing, fighting.) but was stopped by another blow. With blurry eyes, Boy saw the woman tut, shaking her head. She steadied her pistol, tilted her head to the side. The gun clicked.

Boy woke up with a cry caught in his throat. It took him a moment to remember his surroundings. He was alive. It was midday. He had officially run out of food and water. Not great circumstances. Whatever, he dismissed. He could work with it. Still shaken from his nightmare, he got back to work. He hurried through his check of the area. Once completed with only a minor scare because of his own post-dream paranoia, Boy began to pace. Boy began to think.

With his hunters still most likely in the town, he couldn't get supplies till nightfall. His stomach churned at the thought, sharp flashes of pain shooting through his gut. His throat burned for water. He could try, search around the vicinity to see if he could find anything. If he was lucky, maybe he'd find some fruit on a tree. It wasn't likely- most wild plant life had been destroyed in The End but it would be his best bet if he wanted to eat before tomorrow.

Unfortunately, an hour or so later, Boy was back where he started. Standing in the cave, starving, dehydrated and with nothing to do for hours until the embrace of night took hold of the world once again. How fun. Boy let his back hit the cave wall and sank until he could pull his knees to his chest and tug at his hair. Something felt wrong. Something felt very, very wrong. He just couldn't quite put his finger on it.

If there was one thing Boy prided himself on, it was his intelligence. Which is why it felt like a slap across his face when he couldn't crack the plummeting feeling in his stomach. Think, he urged himself, think. The thought rose up and down in his head, as faint as a whisper of the wind. Thinkthinkthink.

How often was it he was in this situation? Once a month? Once a week? He should be used to it by now. An almost second nature. Survival was the one thing he had involuntarily based his entire existence around. So why couldn't he just think?

Soft footsteps came from outside the cave. Boy froze. A short whisper followed, a deep male voice murmuring in a prayerful tone. A religious person? No, a religious hunter. Boy hoped that whatever deity he worshipped was merciful. He doubted it. As a child, Boy had sobbed himself to sleep every night, curled up and shivering in the harsh cold, whispering to whoever was out there in the vast universe, that the game would be over. That he'd wake up and be free. Now, Boy was too old for such fantasies. He'd learned to rattle his chains and sing in his cage. Only five years left to go. And he would survive no matter what. This world wasn't meant for him. That didn't mean it could get rid of him. But for now, he had to run. In the immediate now, he needed to get rid of the other man.

Boy's fingertips itched. He searched for his club, heartbeat slowing as he felt the curved metal handle. He had a knife tucked in his pocket also. His club was more useful. He edged towards the entrance of the cave, back still firmly pressed against the wall. The shadow of the man curled around the corner, his head bowed. In prayer? Seeking blessings in his attempts to find him perhaps. The question was why he was there. Sheer luck?

His hand falling to rest on his club, Boy cupped his other hand around his mouth and whistled. He quickly ducked away, watching as the shadow twisted in alarm. It grew in size and the soft footsteps returned, getting closer. Boy pulled his club out swiftly as the footsteps grew louder, rounding the corner in a sharp movement, his club making contact with the man's chest. The man let out a surprised cry, falling to the ground and landing with a thud. Boy raised his club again and the man shut his eyes. He brought it down. The man fell unconscious. Boy lunged for his shoulders, struggling to pull the man inside. He was heavy. Broad shoulders and awkward limbs that refused to move in a cooperative manner. When he woke up, it would be with bruises. Boy wished he could make himself care.

The man wore a thick coat with small, thin pockets hidden in every seam. Boy rifled through as many as he could, chucking their contents all over the cold stone he knelt on. A prayer book, some coins, a battered photo of a little girl, and more useless sentimental drivel. He found some berries tucked into a corner that lasted only seconds before being hungrily devoured. But nothing else. The man didn't seem to be a threat.

Looks could be deceiving. Boy took out his dagger. He gripped the worn handle tightly, waiting patiently for when the man woke up. He'd interrogate him; find out what exactly he knew. He flicked idly through the prayer book, searching for the most torn and beaten page- his reading skills were limited but he trusted himself to manage to recite a small passage, but didn't find one. Dead end. He could still use the picture. He studied it intently. The man bore similarities to the girl, mostly likely her father. Same brown hair, freckles over the nose. She was important to him. Important enough to warrant carrying the picture around anyway. Good. He could use that.

Slowly but surely, the man began to stir. He groaned as the beams of light hit his eyes. Boy launched from his squatting position to press the dagger snuggly to his neck. The man could feel it but it wasn't drawing blood as he breathed. The feeling of cool metal pressing against his Adam's apple made the man jolt upwards with a cry caught in his throat. His eyes darted, panicked and wide. Boy clicked his tongue.

'Struggling won't get you anywhere.' He said. His voice sounded odd. Barely above a whisper, a croak. He didn't recognize it. 'I won't hurt you. Anymore anyway. Sorry about that. Just calm down for a minute.'

The man squirmed, fear in his eyes. He nodded frantically. Boy smiled grimly.

'Now, what were you doing outside?'

The man shook his head wildly, head swinging violently. 'Nothing!'

'Do they know where I am?'

'Who? Who would care about your whereabouts?' The man squawked, 'Are you a criminal or something?'

Boy rolled his eyes. There were very few people who didn't know who he was. Unfortunately. The crumbling government had put a bounty of 50,000 coins on his head by the time he was four, like they had with all others with abilities before him. They had issued statements and pictures and all sorts of things. Until they had completely worn, little more than shreds, Boy had kept a handful of the posters of the others that came before him in his backpack. He still repeated their names while doing menial tasks, simply to remember them. They hadn't actual names, but Boy named them himself. The nameless blonde boy with a birthmark beside his ear and control over sound became 'Grey'. The blonde girl with the furious eyes and a body that could light like a match, 'Storm'. Once their bounties had been collected, the rest of the world had conveniently forgotten them.

Boy picked up the picture and gazed at it. The man watched him warily, tracking his every movement. Boy held the photo in front of the man, pausing to gauge his reaction. It was subtle. His nostrils flared in a quick and small movement. Before the man could react further, Boy dropped his knife and tore the picture slightly.

The man lunged forwards. Boy quickly returned his dagger to his throat. 'Now we're getting somewhere. Is this your daughter? She's a cute kid.' He paused. 'Tell me, she's, what, three? Four?'

The man struggled against him. A yes. 'Is she still alive?' The man jerked. Another yes. Boy grinned. 'Lucky you. She's in a safe place? You know, I wonder what she'd think if she knew her father wanted to kill another kid for money.'

'You're not a child.' The man blurted.

'But you admit you want to kill me,' asked Boy dryly. The man had an unreadable expression. 'I'll ask again. Do they know where I am?'

The man mumbled in a foreign language, something between cursing him and praying. Boy clicked his tongue, miming a clock. The man didn't respond, squeezing his eyes shut and whispering more passionately. Boy scoffed. He repeated the question.

The man cracked an eye open. 'You wouldn't kill me.'

'No?' asked Boy. The man cocked his head. A small meaningless gesture but Boy was reminded of a wolf, ferocious, patronizing and growling.

Moments later, Boy, having gathered his things and restrained the man quickly, set off towards the town. The hunters could find the man whenever. He needed food, clothes and fast. He needed to get out of here. He'd let himself show weakness to the very people who could kill him for it. Or maybe that was the idea. The man may have just been a decoy by whoever sent him- the blondes? But if that was it the case, it meant...

Boy turned back sharply. Dark clouds rolled across the skies, the sky splitting open as rain crashed to earth. He felt his breath hitch in his throat. He had underestimated the blondes drastically. That was probably the intention. Fear spread from his head to his toes, his breathing becoming erratic. Raindrops dripped down his face.

He couldn't return to the cave. He couldn't face seeing the man's face. The blondes had probably sent another scout that way if they knew what they were doing anyway. He couldn't go to the town as the blondes themselves most likely lay in wait. The next town wasn't for miles. It would take him at least a week to reach it. He wouldn't make it. How could he have been so stupid! The timing of the blondes' arrival couldn't be a coincidence. The engine last night was a test to see if he had reached the town yet. Every small detail unravelled in his mind. The question was now, where could he go?

Boy chewed anxiously on his lip. Relax, He told himself. You just need to think of a plan. He weighed his options over and over again, trying to convince himself to weed out the lesser of the two evils. Unfortunately, or luckily, depending on the viewpoint, Big didn't have to make that decision for himself. A sharp pain suddenly blossomed at the back of his neck. A dart- a tranquilizer.

Boy attempted to pluck the dart from his neck before the liquid entered his bloodstream. He couldn't reach it. The angle was too awkward. So Boy decided to do what he did best. He began to run.

He didn't make it very far, about half a kilometre before drowsiness took over. He stumbled, tripping over thin air and plummeting into the ashy terrain. As the world darkened, Boy wondered if the others before him felt this helpless before they were killed.

Boy woke up in a dimly lit room. Restraints around his wrists and around the chair back. He struggled against them, overcome with panic. The rope wasn't tight but it wasn't loose, a shaky harmony between the two achieved effectively. A small mercy.

He slumped down, squeezing his eyes shut. He wanted to run, he itched to run. He heard shuffling and quiet murmurs in a room beyond the one he was currently in. Could he nudge out his dagger in his pocket? He tried. No luck. His fingers curled in an attempt to unravel the knots binding his wrists. He strained to listen to the muttering in the other room.

'This wasn't a good idea,' said a low voice. It sounded almost familiar. A good familiar. It didn't send a chill down his spine.

'Trust me. When have I ever doubted you?' replied another. There was a soft laugh. Floorboards creaked, weight shifted and cold air hit Boy's face as the door opened. He relaxed his eyes, faking unconsciousness, slowing his movements until they couldn't be recognized. Fear roared in ears like a tidal wave.

A harsh fabric brushed against Boy's shoulder. He felt the floor shake, rickety and poorly made, as the person strode across the room. There was a scrape of wood against wood. Knees brushed against Boy's and stayed there. Silence.

The final knot came apart in Boy's hands. His eyes flew open and he lunged for the person opposite him. They crashed against a wall. Boy raised a fist, curling his thumb inside and brought it down. The woman narrowly avoided the blow, ducking under his arm, grabbing it, twisting it. Boy bit back a cry as pain blossomed through his wrist. He shifted his weight onto one foot, using the other to swipe at her stomach. His knee made contact. He threw a punch.

There was a curse. Boy didn't know who said it. The woman shouted, 'A little help!' throwing a jab at his cheek. There was a crash in the other room. Boy stumbled back out of the way. A pair of hands grabbed his arms, pulling them tight behind his back. Boy yelped. He threw his head back, messily head-butting the person behind him. It didn't work. He was forced back into his chair; his restraints back on only one arm, but tighter.

'That's what I get for being nice I suppose.' The woman sighed, nursing her cheek. She sat back down in her own seat. The man moved to stand beside her. Now that he saw them, he couldn't believe his eyes.

They were both in their early to mid twenties. The woman had long blonde hair, pulled back into a knot at the top of her head. Her eyes were a fierce grey, like a storm cloud was trapped inside of them. The boy had a large birthmark beside his ear and a mop of curly blonde hair on his head. Stood before him were Storm and Grey, two of the kids with abilities who had died when Boy was just a scared six-year-old wondering why he hadn't a home.

'I was hoping you might know who we are. We're…'

'Like me.' Boy finished. 'I know who you are. I mean, I don't know your names but…'

The man Boy had always called 'Grey' smiled. 'Our reputations precede us?'

Boy didn't answer. His shoulders felt tense. Storm (it's not her actual name, he reminded himself.) pulled a chipped glass full of water from under her chair. She held it out. A peace offering.

'Apologies for the tranquilizer. You would have run if we approached you normally. And we both saw you take down our scout. You've got nice knots, by the way. He couldn't get out of them. I had to cut him free. We were hoping you could hear us out. Boy took the glass. He'd listen for now. He was still wary, unease rolling in his stomach, but shrinking by the minute. 'My name is Amelia. This guy's Ethan.' Amelia paused. 'Do you have a name?'

He shook his head. Both tilted their heads slightly, a small sympathetic gesture.

'That's fine. We didn't have any either until a few years back. I'm guessing if you know of us, you know everyone thinks we're dead. And you're probably wondering why we aren't. That's why we wanted to talk to you,' said Amelia.

'To make a long story short, we can offer you freedom. No conditions, no tricks.' said Ethan.

Boy raised his eyebrows. 'That's not a promise you can keep.'

'I know. You shouldn't believe us. But, we're still alive, aren't we? We travelled together while our bounties were still active. The only two left- until you were born, of course. After a run in with some hunters that left us near dead, a group of people found us. Took us in. They're from an organization, based on an island, off the coast of a land further west. Off the radar. Not on any map. They're like us. Most of them, anyway. Your thing's engines, right? They can help you learn to control it there. Harvest it. Not get caught. I mean, I don't turn into a human candle every five minutes now.' Amelia shot to her feet. 'You don't have to run anymore. Not ever. All we want to do is help. But you shouldn't trust us, should you? Because for all you know, we could be lying.'

'Let's say I do believe you. If it's not me, there'll be others,' pointed out Boy.

'We'll find them. No one gets left behind. I promise you,' Ethan said.

'Listen, this is crazy. You're fast and hard to catch- kudos on that by the way- but it only takes one mistake. Are you coming with us? If we set off tomorrow, we'll reach the island in a week. You can have a name. Food. Water. Safety. No more running.' Amelia stared at him. She saw right through him. 'Give it some thought. All up to you.'

Boy swallowed thickly, gaze falling to the floor. It sounded too good to be true. He shouldn't trust a word they said. He should take time to think this over, take into account every variable. But his gut told him to go. They were right there. Living, breathing. Not dead like the hunters had said as they seethed over missing their shot at their bounties. They were tall and strong, not scrawny and starving. They were alive.

If there was one thing Boy prided himself on, it was his intelligence. Survival was priority. This was an opportunity to not only survive, but also thrive. No more hiding. No more hesitation.

His eyes met theirs. 'I'm in.'

He'd be a fool not to take the chance.

Apartment 4A

By Nikoleta Kogan, age 14.

I sit on the worn-out, maroon-black couch:
My grandmother's apartment;
Floor 2, Apartment 4A.

The bulky television displays the old Russian cartoons
with their static-like sound and washed-out colours
– their exaggerated music.
The breeze of July flows gently alongside the sunlight;
Through the balcony, making a soft rustling.

The fiddle-footed budgie chirps and hops around the white wire cage.
All is silent but the budgie and the static.

Nostalgia swallows me whole as a snake its prey.

Where The GAA Calls Home

By Cormac Delaney, age 15.

Off we went to Brownsgrove,
The leaders of our group,
All of us hoping that tomorrow,
We'd be the féile winning troop.

As our feet crunched up the gravel driveway,
School friends run up to greet
But all they meet are enemies,
Determined against defeat.

Soon the 'refs' whistle was ringing in our ears,
The match had started,
Who would be going through?
To the biggest final of the year?

At half-time we were all in a frown,
The blazing hot sun had tired us out,
We were four-nil down,
But we weren't going without a shout.

On we came again with new hope in our hearts
And we started scoring right from the start,
But every time we scored, the opposition scored too,
Until it finally ended by them winning by just few.

Afterwards, the heartbreaking sound of crying
And the sweet aroma of tasty buns
Celebrations for Cortoon, they were qualifying,
Heartbreak yet again, for Caltra fathers and their sons.

But perhaps there will come a day,
When a Caltra team, not including me,
Will get to a féile final,
And defeat Salthill B.

But as we left Cortoon that day
In our green & blue
We left there, both teams the same way
Both teams united, Galway men as true.

We left there that day
In our green and blue, some black, some white
Everyone there, different in their own way.
Everyone there together, without any spite.

The spirit we had inside us
Of our national game,
That spirit we have inside us,
Makes us all the same.

No matter of our differences
We will never stand alone
Because it's what's in our hearts that truly counts,
A place where the GAA calls home.

Decisions

By Úna Duffy, age 15.

Chapter 1

Every decision made in this story is arguably a terrible one.

The sound of footsteps echoed around the room and a tall man with dark skin and ruffled clothes turned and smiled.

'Nice to see you're still alive,' Cassiel said.

'Go to hell.' Uriel replied.

'Been there, done that. Devil didn't like me and sent me back.'

'Of course he didn't; and you were locked out of heaven a long time ago, weren't you? You never were a very good choir boy.' Uriel grinned at Cassiel's eye roll.

'Heaven's overrated. They all pretend they're holy up there. Much more interesting on Earth. There's so much life; drama, redemption, love, hate. Everyone's so busy here, always doing something, creating little legacies. They do so much in their short little lives, so much more than any of us "divine" beings.'

'That sounds bitter.'

Cassiel frowned. 'They were made to survive, not create.'

'They did always have to go against what they were told.'

'It's only logical to them, I know.'

'Of course, you have quite the obsession with them, don't you? These humans.'

'I find them interesting.'

'Interest takes up a few years, decades if you're dedicated. You've been watching over humanity since your creation. That's dedication.'

'That was my job.'

'I'm told there is someone that's been holding your attention too.'

'The purest soul since Eve.'

'Even corruption can't get to it. But a pure soul is a cursed soul. Tragedy falls on it like rain.' Uriel prodded.

'Tragedy befalls everyone, even us,' Cassiel shot back.

'But you're still going to stand by it?'

'Until it can find peace, yes. Why are you here, Uriel?'

'That times coming, Cassiel. He's not walking away from this, and you'll follow him back to heaven.'

'So what? Not my problem.'

'Of course it is. They are running from you.'

'Lots of people run from me. Charlie blames it on my ability to appear without warning.'

'Charlie?' said Uriel.

'You really didn't bother learning his name?'

'Well, he wasn't really the person I was interested in.'

'I'm blushing.'

'You've still got support, up in heaven. They still respect you.'

'I don't want their help,' Cassiel insisted.

'So proud. Or stupid.'

'Guess we'll see. You're the person who's given the girl the spell for the Queens, aren't you?'

Uriel's smile dropped. A phone started ringing, the sound echoing against the concrete walls in the empty room, and Cassiel pulled it out of his pocket and answered. 'Hello? I'm fine, just met an old friend. No, of course you don't know them— Duty's calling. I'm finished with handing out spells so no need to send the dogs. I'm sure we'll see each other around.' He nodded. 'I'm coming back now. Goodbye.'

Both angels nodded to each other and Cassiel took off, the sound of wings echoing in the silence.

'Heavens, they're going to get themselves killed. Or me, I guess.' Uriel spread his wings and flew away too. Leaving another echo of wings.

Chapter 2

Charlie frowned as he shovelled his clothes into a bag. 'An old friend?'

'Yes, we were trained together.' Cassiel shifted a pile of books aside and picked up one.

'Oh well, sorry for interrupting you.'

He didn't look up as he flicked through the pages. 'It's fine, it wasn't anything important. Just crossing streams.'

'Well okay then.' Charlie shoved another shirt into his bag and glanced at Cassiel out of the corner of his eye. 'What's their name?'

Cassiel glanced up from the book in surprise. 'What? Oh, eh, Uriel.'

'Like the angel of love and protection?' Oliver perked up peering up from where he was lying on the bed with Hela, looking at his laptop as she sharpened a blade.

'Yes, he is known as that. He's a lot more "rebellious" than you're led to believe.'

'Oh, and what's rebellious? Playing his harp too loud? Flying over the speed limit?' He grinned at Cassiel.

'He may be the reason the Queens are on Earth.'

'Seriously?! And you let him go? That could have been our chance to end this!'

Cassiel frowned and took a step towards where Charlie was glaring at him.

'We're not killing him, Charlie.'

Charlie faltered at Cassiel's tone and sighed, 'I, I know but you could have brought him here or told us and we would have met you there.'

'I didn't get the chance. I thought you had called about the Queens, so I left.' Cassiel's voice hardened as he stayed where he was.

'We do but… ' Charlie ran his hand through his hair before turning back to his bag. 'Whatever.'

'We found something that will send the Queens back to wherever they came from.' Oliver took over pushing himself up, his prosthetic arm holding the laptop up to Cassiel.

'They come from the in-between.' Hela piped up, pulling some of her hair back from her face.

'Huh. Well, we need a golden blade soaked in rosewater and tar.'

Cassiel looked away from Charlie and nodded. 'I'll go get a blade.'

Charlie looked up and turned to Cassiel. 'Hey, wait- And he's gone. Great.' He threw a pair of jeans on the bed and dropped onto the floor beside Oliver.

'Maybe you should text him and ask for him to get more than one blade. Or else we'll end up playing a demented game of hot potato.'

Chapter 3

'Angels are so stuck up. They think they're so important just because they've been around since the start.' Hela whined, stretching over the edge of the crappy motel bed, her wings folded neatly under her, her short hair sticking out.

'Of what?' Oliver looked over at her curiously, his seat on the ground beside her head cluttered with pages and books.

'I dunno? Everything? They're not the chattiest bunch.'

'…Yeah… I still can't say Cassiel tells me everything. Or anything about his relationships with other angels.' Charlie sipped at his drink and kicked the leg of a chair. His own brown hair was cropped short, harder to be grabbed in a fight; ever practical.

'And he's the friendliest I've met in decades,' said Hela.

'Who was the last?'

Hela grabbed one of the books and peered at it. 'Gabriel.'

'The archangel?'

'Yeah, cool guy. He was trying to lay low among some other Valkyries though; so maybe not so innocent.' She tossed the book back on the ground and grinned at Oliver's glare.

'Doesn't solve the question of who exactly the angel Cassiel met with was, or why they were giving out "catch your own queen" recipes.'

'Or where either of them are.'

'Maybe you could ask him.' Cassiel mocked, standing at the door.

'It would never work.'

'Hela.' Charlie warned, pushing himself up off the floor. 'Where is he?'

'I don't know.'

'Why's he giving teenage dumbasses ways to find the Queens?'

'Bite me, oldie.' The teenager tied to a chair hissed.

'Watch it.'

Charlie kicked the chair leg again.

'I didn't ask.' Cassiel said, eyes trained on the girl as she glared at Charlie.

'Did you ask him anything?'

'I asked why he was here.'

'And what? He didn't immediately spill his master plan?'

'No…. he-' Cassiel cut himself off and shook his head.

'What?'

'It's not important. Preaching.'

'About what?'

'Angels.' He pulled the golden blades out of his coat and put them on the table. 'They think I'm going to return.'

'And they're… angry?' Oliver asked, pushing himself up.

'Worried.'

'About what?'

'I was one of the most respected angels in heaven before joining you.' Cassiel frowned and started pulling out the tar and rosewater. 'Apparently, I'm still considered one.'

'You're willing just to believe this guy? Just like that?'

'I've known Uriel a long time Charlie.'

'I've known Hela for the last three years and I still won't trust her around an open drink!'

'One-time, dude. It was an accident!'

'He has said he's done with giving out spells, don't start on that again.'

Hela grinned at Charlie and raised an eyebrow. 'Really it's your own fault for drinking the first brown liquid you saw in the morning.'

Chapter 4

'Let's just question the girl, okay?' Oliver stepped between the two before Charlie could respond. Charlie shot her another glare over his head.

'"The girl" has a name.' the teenager scowled at the three as they stepped towards her.

'It's Suzy.' Hela said immediately.

'What? No, it's—'

'Not important,' Charlie interrupted. 'Why were you summoning the Queens?'

'I was cursed by a witch. I needed to find a way to break it.'

'All right, what does the curse do to you? Cause you're looking pretty good for a marked woman.'

'Two days every month I get turned into some sort of monster or beast or something.'

'And that needed Queen summoning power to deal with?' Hela asked, scepticism dripping from her voice.

'What; a werewolf?' Oliver asked, looking at the other two.

'No, lycanthropy can't be cursed on someone, only passed on by genetics or by a bite.' Hela answered, frowning.

'Huh, Skinwalker?'

'Not passed or acquirable by curse.'

'And you keep your head when you turn?' Charlie asked Suzy, who was watching them from her chair at the other side of the room.

'Yeah, mostly.' she answered with a frown.

'Sounds a lot like a Skinwalker to me, even if she can't control it. How was the first one created? Maybe that's what's happened?'

'That would be a question for the Queen of Monsters.'

'She created all monsters?'

'No one's sure how anything was made, but the Queens have the most extensive knowledge and control over their subjects.'

There was a rustle and Cassiel appeared in the centre of the room, his shirt rumpled and coat on his arm.

'I've found one of the Queens.'

'Which one?'

'She had a snake?'

'Serpents. Not the worst for our first Queen.'

'Great.' Charlie turned to Suzy and nodded. 'You're staying here.'

'What? You can't do that!'

'Yeah, I can. You got people killed.'

Hela frowned at Suzy and raised an eyebrow. 'You're lucky that you're alive honestly.'

Chapter 5

The warehouse was surprisingly small. Really it was more of a big storage unit. And it was filthy. Oliver frowned as he looked around, running a finger across one of the boxes beside him.

'There has to be somewhere cleaner to do this.'

'I wasn't exactly spoiled for choice; this place was closest, and there obviously hasn't been anyone here in years.'

'That's one way to put it.'

Their voices were dulled by the dust and boxes as they walked further into the musty room.

The Queen of Serpents was standing in the centre of a binding circle as they rounded the corner.

'I demand to be released!' She demanded, stepping closer to the edge of the circle. Her eyes flicked between the four before landing on Charlie. She smiled and edged closer the outer lines of the binding circle.

'My snake in the garden; I've heard lots about you.'

'Oh, great.'

'You're also the next Eve. Light can't wait to get her hands on you.'

'What?' Oliver frowned and stepped closer to the Queen. Hela raised a hand to grab him, but stopped and let it drop back to her side.

'The angel must know, boy's got a soul like a lighthouse.'

Charlie looked at Cassiel, who frowned at the smug Queen.

'No one's putting any hands on Charlie.'

'Not to mention that her full name is Queen of Light and Cruelty. Not so friendly sounding.' Hela added, giving Charlie a tight smile.

'A lot of judgement for a Valkyrie.'

'Just the right amount of judgement I'd say.'

The silence lingered as the two women stared each other down.

'What did you mean by snake in the garden?'

The Queen blinked in surprise and looked at Oliver with a frown.

'Every few hundred years or so a soul comes along that's truly pure.'
Oliver took another step towards her. 'Your brother is the purest to come
along since Eve.'

'Like, the first woman, Eve?'

'Not the first, but sure.'

'And the snake is from the same story?'

'Well done, you get a cookie.'

'So, I'm the snake and Eve? That doesn't even make sense.' Charlie butted
in defensively.

'We all know that. That's why light wants you; she wants to see what
makes you tick. And Fates wants you to stop dodging your fate.'

'Once again, that's not happening.' Cassiel pulled out his blade.

'One of you'll get him killed. Or he'll get himself killed; guess we'll see.'

Oliver took a third step forwards, scuffing the chalk on the floor. 'Why?'

The Queen grinned and Hela jerked forwards, but she had already grabbed
him and pulled away from the circle. Snakes began tumbling out of her
dress, making their way to Cassiel and Hela as they tried to grab her. She
grinned and pushed Oliver away, before turning and coming face-to-face
with Charlie.

'If that's all you have to say, I'd like to finish this.'

He plunged the blade into her chest and twisted. Symbols rose to the surface of her skin and he yanked the knife out of her heart, stumbling away from her now-glowing body. One of the Queen's snakes snapped at him, digging its fangs into his arm. He screamed and plunged the knife into its body.

Chapter 6

Hela grabbed Charlie and suddenly they were back in the motel room, Cassiel following quickly with Oliver.

'Okay; Charlie? I'm going to have to draw out the venom before Cassiel can heal you. This is gonna hurt.'

Hela turned and sighed when she saw Oliver. 'Oli, it's okay. I'm just removing the venom and he'll be good.'

'Right, yeah. I'll grab your stuff.'

'And the first aid kit please.' She added, turning back to Charlie and helping Cassiel pull him into a sitting position on the bed. Hela pulled a knife from thin air and tore Charlie's shirt sleeve off around the wound and slowly removed the fabric. The snake had torn away at his skin and blood was leaking out of it sluggishly.

'Well at least it didn't hit a vein.' She muttered, shoving everything off the cluttered nightstand beside the bed.

Oliver returned to the bed with an old leather satchel and a first aid bag with a suspiciously blood-like stain covering most of one side. Hela grabbed the satchel and began pulling out bottles and herbs and a small bowl that she began throwing various plants and powers into.

'Water, please.' she asked, as smoke began rising, filling the room with the smell of tulips and arsenic.

Cassiel grabbed a bottle and handed it to her. Hela held the bowl under Charlie's wound, blood dripping into it as she added the water. There was a hiss and Hela dumped the churning contents of the bowl onto the wound before throwing herself onto him and pinning to the bed. Charlie let out a strangled scream and tried to fling himself out of the bed; Cassiel grabbed him and pushed him back down.

Chapter 7

Oli studied Cassiel's expression as they sat at the table, eating crappy gas-station food. He was frowning at a dent on the metal of the table.

'Do you know anything about what the Queen of Serpents was saying?'

Cassiel looked up and stared at Oli. Green and blue eyes locked and Oliver could practically see the power stirring just behind them.

'Yes.'

'Why didn't you say anything?'

'It's not relevant. Like she said, there is one every few hundred years.'

'She also said Charlie was different! What about that?'

'Sometimes people just say things, Oli. She was trying to get you close enough to break the circle.' Hela spoke up, obviously trying to calm the situation before anyone started yelling.

'Charlie does appear to be exceptional. Most pure souls instinctively try to stay that way, and avoid the things that your brother seeks out.' Cassiel frowned as he looked at Charlie. 'That's why he's the snake; he's trying to taint his own soul.'

'And when were you going to mention any of this?!' Oliver was furious, he hated being left out of the loop and Charlie's injury seemed to have shaken him more than either of them thought.

'It's hardly your business! I told Charlie exactly why Michael had been assigned to him, and his decision not to tell you isn't my problem.'

The two had ended up standing toe to toe, Cassiel glaring down at the short man, and they both froze when Charlie cleared his throat from the bed.

'Seriously guys?'

Cassiel stepped back and Hela pushed by them and passed Charlie a bottle of water.

'I've a lead on the Queen of Fates and Lost Things. She's the ringleader of the attacks; so if we get her most of the others will leave on their own.'

'When we heading out?'

'Tonight.'

'He can't go! You've just been bit!' Oli insisted.

'So? I'm fine now, look.' Charlie lifted his arm and made a noise of surprise at the scars on his forearm.

'They'll mostly fade. Bites from the Queen's snakes won't ever fully heal, even if you survive.' Hela explained, picking up the bowl she had left on the bed and shoving it into a bag. The room had been packed while Charlie was sleeping and Suzy was now untied and sitting on the couch, watching the scene play out.

'What's she doing free?' He demanded, trying to stand up, while Hela put a hand on his shoulder.

'It's finally sunk in that people are getting hurt and she's going to try and live with it instead of going after more Queens.'

'Fat lot of good that'll do now.' Charlie grabbed his boots and pulled them on, ignoring the cut on Suzy's cheek that wasn't there before.

'We may as well leave now; it won't change anything.'

They threw their bags into the back of the van and Charlie glared at Oliver when he went to sit up front.

'No. Hela's going to sit in the front and you three are going to sit in the back.'

'Seriously? Dude, come on.' Oli argued throwing him a pleading look.

'No. Maybe you should have thought about this when you let her pull you in and you broke the circle.' He climbed into the driver's seat. 'Don't let one of them get to you again.'

Chapter 8

'I haven't actually got her trapped or anything; a friend just tipped me off that Fates had been hanging around in Clanton in Alabama.'

'How long should it take to get there?'

'I'm guessing about six hours? We'll be there before sunrise.'

'Great. You guys should get some sleep. We're going to have to swap out at some point.'

Hela woke up in the back of the van. Charlie had swapped with Cassiel and she had moved to the back to let them sit together. She could hear the quiet conversation they were having, even over the rattling and roaring of the engine as they flew down the motorway.

'— even if that's true, who cares? I would never have settled for a normal life.'

Cassiel didn't take his eyes off the road as he spoke. 'I know that, I'm just relaying what he said. Though I don't believe Fate would have ever given you a normal life. Even the angels called you the fated slayer.'

'Seriously? That's so pretentious.'

'It's certainly not one of the things I miss about being there.'

'Do you miss it? Heaven?'

Cassiel frowned, flicking the headlights up the illuminate the barren, pitch black road. All you could see was the tarmac pilling up behind them. 'I miss some of the people. And seeing the young angels learn to fly, I guess.'

Charlie looked sad as Cassiel spoke.

'I spent most of my time on Earth anyways. Joshua asked me to dedicate myself to watching the universe's creations, and I loved my job.'

'Sounds like a lonely existence, if I'm honest.' Charlie commented quietly.

Cassiel laughed in response. 'That was my nickname.'

'The lonely angel.'

Chapter 9

They arrived in Clanton around 5:30 am and decided to book a motel and wait it out until that night to go after the Queen of Fates. Their motel room was small and dingy and they had to get two as compensation. The room they were in at present had murky brown wallpaper, water staining across most of the roof, and a bathroom that definitely wasn't up to code, with something growing in the corner of the shower and a counter that was warm and slimy to touch.

It was 7:30 and the four were preparing to go to the house Cassiel and Hela had followed a worshipper of the Queen's to earlier in the day. The air was thick with tension and every movement had the hair on the back of Charlie's neck stand up straight and he shivered.

'That can't just be me.' He rubbed his arms as goosebumps ran up his forearm.

'Huh?' Hela looked up, distracted. 'It's Fates, she's definitely here...'

Oliver furrowed his brows, 'What's up?'

'I'm just fine tuned to fates, and being this close to the Queen is.... Overwhelming.'

'Do you think she knows that we're here?'

Cassiel shook his head. 'Not yet. She'll know when we're closer.'

'Comforting.' Suzy muttered.

'You're not coming anyways. You'll just piss her off.'

The townhouse was grand and would be extremely inviting if it wasn't for the hooded figures pacing past the windows and standing sentry at the doors. Two were standing at the door, obviously trying to look casual, one of them was smoking and they were talking quietly; even as they scanned the area.

'Best thing is probably to have me and Cassiel fly you in and that way we can avoid a complete bloodbath.'

'Or you could just go through the front door?'

They all whipped around, pulling out their blades. Standing in front of them was a woman. Well, the shape of a woman. She was surrounded by an inky blackness that shifted like ripples in water, with small, dark flowers growing like hair from her head and larger ones covering her in a colourful myriad of blooms. Her voice sounded like it was coming from right beside your ear in a soft whisper, like a leaf brushing by you on a windy day.

'Queen of Darkness and Flowers.' Hela muttered, awe painted across her face, the knife held loosening in her hand.

'I'm not here to fight.' she placated. 'My… fellow Queens are being unreasonable.'

They were sure that if they could actually see her face she would be frowning as well as looking off to the side as she was now.

'The Queen of Fates and Lost Things already knows you're coming. There's no point in trying to sneak in.'

'And how would she know that?' Charlie snapped, obviously not impressed by her attempt to calm their concerns.

'You.' The Queen snapped back, her head turning to him, her unseen eyes digging into his soul. 'Being anywhere near you causes an unbelievable amount of your possible fates to start forming and collapsing, like towers made of sand and dust.'

She gave the small group a mocking bow and stepped back into the shadows and disappeared.

'I guess we're taking the direct route in.

The carpet was so plush they sunk into it every time their feet hit the ground and the hall they were walking through was filled with pointless tables with empty ornate vases and unimpressive paintings that probably cost more than the house itself. The only sound was quiet talking from a room at the end of the long hallway that the two people from the front door were leading them down. The last door at the end of the hall opened and a group of robed people filed out, along with two women who Hela quietly identified as the Queen of Dreams, and Lightning and Sound, respectively. The first Queen spoke softly and had a glazed, faraway look that gave you goosebumps if seen at the right angle; seemingly permanently fixed on her face. It became clear as she passed that her feet weren't even touching the ground. The other Queen was like a polar opposite, her voice echoing in a booming tone around the hall and sharp, flashing eyes, offset by a scar of forked lightning travelling down her cheek and onto her right arm. When she passed them all the hair on their arms and necks stood up and their skin crawled.

Once the doorway was free they headed inside and were greeted with the Queen of Fates standing at the head of a large table. It was covered with a large map that showed where there had been natural disasters or strange deaths. The Queen of Fates and Lost Things herself was wearing a golden threaded tunic and long skirt that had a long scabbard holding a dao, similar to Hela's own, tied around her waist.

'Oh, wonderful. You're here.' She straightened and tilted her head. 'Why on earth would an angel and two monster slayers work with a Valkyrie?' She strode closer to them and smirked. 'Is she your pet?'

Hela smiled and tilted her head down to look at the Queen. 'Your plan is to make fun of me?'

'My plan is to kill you actually. I was just curious as to how you ended working with these barbarians.'

'We're actually quite charming. You should get to know us first.' Cassiel said, stepping forward slightly.

Fates' eyes darkened. 'I'm done with getting to know you three. Every other thing on this earth can just go with fate, not you though, oh no.' She turned to Charlie, 'I'm glad I'm about to finally end your story. It was always going to end bloody, that's all I ever knew after you continually cheated your fates.'

Charlie smirked and raised an eyebrow at the Queen. 'I've always been pretty sneaky.'

There was a glint of metal and the Queen of Fates and Lost Things gasped as a blade pierced her back. Hela pulled out the blade and Charlie lodged his in her chest, twisting it. They all leapt away from her as she lit up and her eyes glowed a deep gold. The golden light enveloped her and she disappeared with a flash, leaving only a scorch mark on the fancy hardwood floor.

They froze when the door opened. Hela didn't need to tell them who it was, the Queen had skin that seemed to be made of pure light and eyes the colour of rust. The suit she was wearing had blood speckled across the front and a long kitchen knife was held in her left hand. Those rusty eyes moved from the scorch mark to the blade dripping gold blood in Charlie's hand and her face twisted in rage.

'What have you done?' she roared, leaping at them.

There was a flicker behind her and suddenly the Queen of Darkness and Flowers was behind Light and holding her around the waist, her arms pinned to her side. Oliver jumped at the opportunity and plunged his blade into her chest. The Queen of Darkness stepped away and watched as the Queen of Light disappeared in a similar fashion.

'I'm taking my leave. Thank you for your work.' The Queen began to glow. 'You'll find a friend in the flowers and darkness, but I hope we never meet again.'

Going willingly seemed to be a lot less of a violent affair as she slowly grew darker until the darkness hurt to look at and when they looked back there was a dark red flower lying on the ground. Hela strode over a plucked it off the ground.

'We ought to get back to the motel, tell Isla the news.'

'Who?'

'You didn't really think her name was Suzy, did you?'

Oliver let out a surprised laugh and shook his head, finally relaxing. 'We should go; someone's going to show up eventually.'

Chapter 10

'It's lashing rain.' Cassiel pointed out, standing at the balcony door. The balcony had a small outdoor table and an old target propped against the wall.

'At least I have an umbrella.' he argued.

'Standing out here's going to make you sick.'

'Well, I can't ignore this lovely weather.' Charlie leaned over the balcony rail and peered down at the street. His umbrella slipped and water ran down the front, falling on the pathway down below.

'Everyone else manages to.' Cassiel stepped out, under the umbrella.

'And look at how the sky weeps for them.' Charlie swung back on the rail and grinned at Cassiel.

'It "weeps" for fools who fall in love with things that can kill them.' He shot back mockingly. Thunder rumbled distantly and a lightning crack echoed through the city.

'Anything could kill you.' The wind whipped around the building and pulled at their clothes.

'So maybe you should stop tempting Fates, she'll literally tear you apart if she finds you.'

Charlie smirked and raised his head. 'Only lost things can be found.'

The sky was dark and the rain lashed down on the buildings around them, blurring them around the edges.

'Charlie, we're all lost things.' Cassiel leaned closer to him.

'Does what the Queen of Fates said to you bother you?'

'About dying bloody?' Cassiel nodded. 'No, most slayers die bloody. It's how it is.'

The lightning flashed closer to their cluttered little balcony.

'Standing outside in a storm with an umbrella is also a surefire way to get electrocuted.'

Charlie jerked away from the rail and Cassiel laughed and led the way back into the apartment.

So maybe not every decision was bad.

Tricked

By Joe Reidy, age 15.

Autumn is a middle aged man
Stuffed in tweed, shuffling to work
Counting the days.

Autumn throws its leaves;
Gives no heed to who will clean
The eaves.

Smart swallows, long gone
To South Africa, their droppings left
On the garage floor.

Veils between worlds, thin
Ghostly voices drowned by kids
High on Haribo.

Autumn is a neon ghoul
Outside the pound shop.
Plastic pumpkins piled on shelves

'Samhain Shona' from China

It's a Hard Knock Life

By Gráinne Beirne, age 15.

I smirked as I watched her. Her face was contorted with humiliation. Her tears threatened to spill. Her cheeks turned an ugly shade of crimson. She struggled to contain her messy hair, falling out of its ponytail.

So I continued.

I rolled my eyes. Even watching her now aggravated me.

'What a baby,' I muttered under my breath. She couldn't even take a small teasing. A meagre hit.

The girl can no longer compose herself as she starts to whimper at my feet. She tucks her bedraggled, matted hair behind her ears to reveal her pasty, white face entirely. Her eyes are cobalt blue and are framed by thick, black-rimmed glasses. Her lips are chapped and she draws more attention to them as she nervously bites on them. She fumbles with her books and in the process her glasses plummet to the ground.

So. I smile coyly.

My name is Britney Walsh. This is my daily routine. Some would call me a bully, but they don't understand that I am trying to help these feeble people. I break them down so that they are prepared for life when it hits them in the face. That's what my dad told me. At first I didn't understand his theory. Every time I endured his cuts and bruises, I tried to see from his point of view, but I was blind to it. But now I know.

So. I am resilient and tough. Nothing can deter me. All thanks to my dad. He has, of course, raised me with my best interests at heart. I should never have doubted him.

'Oh, let me get that for you,' I say, my voice dripping with sweetness. She examines me through squinted eyes, trying to figure out my intention. I step around her with caution, not wanting to be near such scum. I bend down and let my pink, satin heels hover over her bulky glasses. I allow the suspense to build as I hear her breath hitch. I relish the panicked frenzy that overcomes her features. As she grabs for her glasses, I lay my weight down. The satisfying snap echoes throughout the hall. I see a few glances thrown our way, but they hurry on nonetheless. Smirking, I raise an eyebrow.

So. I own this school.

An agonising gasp is audible from the girl's mouth and I take a sharp breath, with my hand placed on my chest. I fix a hurt, sympathetic look on my face.

'Oh my God,' I exclaim, my voice free from emotion, a stark contrast to my previous tone. 'I am so sorry.'

I smile smugly at the now-wailing mess that lies on the floor in front of me, as I saunter down the hallway, my admirers following me.

I hope that she appreciates what I've done for her. She doesn't know how lucky she is. To have someone there for her, like my dad was for me. She doesn't realize it now, but she will.

One day.

My name is Britney Walsh, and I am a bully.

So, as I said.

It's a hard knock life.

Insomniac Maniac

By Tara Mc Gorman, age 14.

Every night;

I feel you,

Creeping up from under my bed.

Like a hidden monster,

You start to creep,

slowly up my body

 From my feet,

to my knees,

to my legs,

to my chest,

to my head,

Fear gripping me.

I can't move.

In the dead of night I hear your silent screams,

Of regret.

Insomnia release me,

Before I drown;

Before I drown in

a sea of thought,

wallowing in remorse,

wallowing in worries,

wallowing in regret
and doubt,

Slowly the light of dawn creeps
 In.
Finally I see the light,
The light of sun.
It burns you,
so you hide away,
     back under my bed.

Glorious morning you have finally arrived,
Like a prince charming.
You have rescued me...

Until tonight when dark falls,
And we see our true selves.

The Stolen Corpse

by Ciara Smyth, age 14.

Elizabeth died.
I was gutted,
mourning her.

A matchstick box to contain her corpse;
her once-vibrant orange scales
fading away,
slowly decomposing.
The box placed within a hole
dug into the moist soil.

A blazing summer day,
I wandered outside.
The dirt once covering the box:
scattered across the yard.

Elizabeth? Gone.

I spotted a girl across the road.

A devilish grin plastered across her face.
I approach cautiously,
scanning for senses of discomfort.

Out of her dense pocket,
within her white knuckled fist,

Elizabeth.

Stimming

By Lucy Hood, age 14.

Colours and pictures shimmer through the vivid landscape of my mind.

Fizzing with ideas for stories, poems or songs, whatever takes my fancy.

Gently I hold these ideas while swathing them in creativity, letting them ripen before delving deeper into them with the power of stimming.

Gaining the deep mysteries of them by flapping in a continual loop, all the while growing excited as my world comes into view.

Faster my arms go, urging my feet to follow, to make a strong rhythm to keep me in my mind.

The ideas are glowing, forming brighter all the time until they're white hot, then gold.

I am wrapped in my brain with my creativity until I am stopped.

Why?

By Ciara Browne, age 14.

It was New Year's Day in the year 2020 when the first case was recorded. It started with one patient and spread rapidly in only a few hours. The first thing that became clear to the doctors was that the virus was contagious, then, that it was airborne and lastly that it had never been seen before. The doctors called the disease 'Manatuto', after the area where it was first discovered. The symptoms begin when the patient suddenly comes down with a flu-like illness. Then the nausea begins and they break out in a rash, then they get a very high temperature. Within three days most of the original victims had died.

When Lily Reynolds walked into the World Health Organization she immediately knew there was something wrong. The corridors were normally quiet this time of the morning, but today they were bustling with life. She had gotten a phone call from Simon telling her she was needed at work as soon as possible. As she walked into the large conference room she noticed a group of doctors huddled over a large computer. Most of them were her colleagues, but some of them she had never seen before. She knew they weren't any doctors; they were the best doctors the world had. Simon Fitzpatrick was an Irish-American genius who was wise beyond his fifty-five years. He ran a hand through his silvery-grey hair, an old habit. 'It's unlike anything we've ever seen before,' he sighed. He showed her the brief he had received from the hospital. Lily felt her heart stop. She could tell from her colleagues' faces that this virus hadn't just appeared. It had been created in a lab and released. But who was responsible?

'Who do you think did it?' Lily asked, her voice barely a whisper. 'At the moment we're considering all possibilities.' Lily nodded her head in agreement. The voice of the secretary interrupted her thoughts, 'Excuse me, but the President would like to make a call.'

'Ok, you can put the call through now,' Simon replied.

'Good,' thought Lily; the president might have some answers.

'Ladies and gentlemen,' the voice of President Jim Spielberg boomed over the speakers. 'My team have come to the conclusion we are dealing with a biological weapon, you all know the consequences of this'.

The doctors nodded their heads in agreement. The President continued 'I need you to send a team over to the infected area to work out who is responsible for this great tragedy'.

Simon replied gravely 'We won't let you down'.

Six hours later Lily was on a plane to Timor along with Simon's team. Vitali Kosgrave a Russian, with deep brown eyes and wispy brown hair, Wanna Chaiyaphum, a Philipino with long hair, black like midnight and a pretty smile and Charles Windsor an elderly Brit with old-fashioned ideas. When they arrived in the quarantined area, they were carefully suited up in airtight gear, they couldn't take any chances. Taking a long, shaky breath Lily entered the ward.

The first thing she noticed was the smell of disinfectant, which was distinct to hospitals. Then she saw it. Patients everywhere, lying on trolleys, beds or the floor. It was a mad scene. Lily's eyes burned with tears. She'd never forget this sight as long as she lived.

It had been four days since she'd first entered the hospital. She'd barely gotten any sleep and it had taken its toll on her. She scraped her long, wavy, caramel-coloured hair into a messy bun and began her fourth coffee of the day. She had been working late into the night reading files, testing patients and trying to work out why this had happened. Suddenly her phone began to ring. It was Simon

'It's Charles,' he said. That was all Lily needed to here. He had caught the virus. He was one of 268 cases that had been recorded since that fateful New Year's Day.

Lily knew that if she didn't find out who was behind this, she could catch the disease. She had to act fast. There was one thing she hadn't checked yet. The first patient's file. It wasn't in the file room, which she found suspicious, but she hadn't had time to think about it. She decided to check the staff room to check in case any other doctors had it. Wanna was sitting there sipping on a cup of tea. Her suspicious eyes looked as tired as Lily felt. Lily discreetly searched the room.

'Looking for something?' Wanna asked in her heavy accent.

'Nothing, nothing at all,' Lily replied. She had never really grown to trust Wanna. There was something about her Lily couldn't quite put her finger on.

Lily went to the lab. The file had to be there. The lab was a dangerous place. The very air was deadly. The room itself was snow white. It was spotless. She looked around the room was full of test tubes and equipment and in the corner nearly out of view was a stack of files. Lily searched for the right one and there it was, in the centre, almost like it was being hidden. Lily's hands trembled with fear, she was terrified of what she would read. When she opened the file and saw what was inside she felt faint. It was her worst fear come to life. It wasn't a foreign government to blame for this outbreak, it was her government.

She needed answers and she had a feeling she knew where to find them.

She ran to Simon's makeshift office. She burst through the door and threw the file onto his desk. Simon took a glance at the file.

'I'd wondered how long it would take you to find this. Wanna mentioned you had been poking around the staff room.'

'Charles found out too you know and we took care of him. Well,' he sighed 'I guess we'll have to take care of you too'. He pulled out a syringe. Lily screamed…

Orange

By Joseph Lalor, age 15.

A fruit the colour of fire,

not quite red,

not quite yellow.

It sets the leaves alight in autumn,

burning the forest to the ground.

It mourns the passing of the night,

with a pyre of clouds every morning.

The colour of melted metal, of all kinds:

tin, lead, gold, iron, copper and silver.

Orange is the colour of all metals,

no matter what they say.

Losing Neverland

By Megan Murrin, age 14.

'I don't want to go, Peter.' Wendy said as she gripped onto his hand.

The darkness was faster now, the thick blackness advancing towards them at an alarming speed.

'I know.' he replied. What else was there to say? They had run for as long as they could until they came face to face with the side of a vast cliff edge. There was nowhere left to go, nowhere left to hide.

John and Michael had been consumed by the darkness long ago, maturity taking the two so much sooner than Wendy.

The darkness wasn't just a thing. It was a being. A living state of mind.

It was adulthood. Wendy was now seventeen and in only a matter of minutes the clock would chime midnight and her eighteenth birthday would finally arrive, meaning she would become the official age of an adult.

This also meant that she would have to grow up and leave fantasies, wonders and dreams behind. Wendy had been living in a certain dream for too long and the darkness was coming to wake her up.

John, her brother, had stopped believing the moment he turned thirteen, and Michael, wanting to follow in his older brother's footsteps, gave up believing too. Wendy still couldn't believe that they both had been taken so soon.

Wendy hadn't stop growing older; she just refused to grow up. Peter, in his natural kindness, had allowed himself to age with her and so he looked like a proper man, his ginger hair unevenly cut, the traditional green suit stretched as far as it could be.

His cheeky grin had never changed though; the same devilish smirk still played with her heartstrings.

For years after the first time they had encountered one another, she had continued to go on many adventures with the boy who wouldn't grow up.

She still held onto the one thing that she truly loved. And so had he.

But the deadline had come. Eighteen years of age and now she was being forced to grow up. They knew that if – no, it was when now – it reached them, it would take the most important thing the two had: their friendship. This darkness was set on wiping away Peter, wiping away all childhood fantasies from Wendy's mind, leaving her a blank slate to become an adult in the horrible mess of a 'grown up world'.

Wendy and Peter had hoped that they would have been able to outrun it, but it was approaching.

'Peter?' said Wendy, fright making her voice high pitched.

He turned to her. There was nothing else they could do.

'You have to leave now,' he said, his head down hiding his face. He wouldn't let her see him like this.

'No,' her voice started as barely a whisper, 'No, no, no!'

Her shouts only then came because she was realising the inevitable truth. That she did have to leave. There was no escaping the future. 'Peter, please,' she begged. 'There must be something else we can do.' The tears that had threatened to spill all this time now perched at her eyelids, her rapid blinking sent them flowing freely down her cheeks. 'I can't leave you.'

Peter looked up. He too had tears, and they were like tiny twin waterfalls, one droplet after the other, each one exposing him and making him feel that much more vulnerable.

He squeezed her hand, looked her in the eyes and smiled. She always did have beautiful eyes.

'You know there's nothing else we can do.' His voice was wobbly, sadness layered into every word.

Wendy was sobbing now and she lowered her head, 'I know.'

He placed a finger under her chin and raised her head, making her look at him. 'Don't leave me in sadness Wendy,' He raised the same hand and wiped a tear that was currently running down her face. 'Remember when we first met?'

She gave him a small smile. 'Of course I do. You broke into our home looking for Shadow. I helped you attach him back.' They both were thinking back to the memory of when neither had any cares, worries or burdens that sat so heavily on their shoulders and held down their worlds.

The sky became overcast and Wendy looked out at the blackness that had been chasing her. It was so much closer now and a chill ran down her spine.

'Hey,' Peter said, putting the attention back on him. 'Eyes on me.'

'I really don't want to go Peter.' she said again, the crack in her voice breaking his heart.

This was it.

Their final moments together.

Before thinking, Wendy put her arms around the neck of the boy she loved and pulled him into the tightest hug ever given. Peter wrapped his arms around her, pulling her close.

He had to let her go soon, but…

'I'll be with you, Wendy, I promise,' he pulled back for a moment to look at her beautiful, elegant face, one that he had loved so dearly for all these years. 'You know that place between sleep and awake; that place where you can still remember dreaming? That's where I'll be waiting. That's where I will always love you.'

His tears spilled and this time he saw no point in trying to hide them. Instead he just let Wendy pull him back into the hug. The two of them wrapped in each other's arms. As they wish it could be forever.

'I love you Peter Pan.' she whispered into his ear.

More tears. More heartbreak.

'I love you more, Wendy Darling.'

And with that, Peter kissed Wendy.

The kiss was sweet, passionate and said thousands of words neither would have been able to express out loud. The kiss held love and true emotions, feelings the two may have hidden.

And, in the moment, Wendy kissed him back. With more love, more sadness, more of a farewell.

When they broke apart for air they found that it was too late for anything more. The darkness was upon them. They turned to each other one last time and with their love so purely displayed, held one another close until the end.

'I will never stop loving you.' Wendy whispered into Peter's ear before the darkness consumed them both.

After what seemed like hours, the dark finally passed on and Peter found himself on his knees.

He saw the tears drop onto the ground before he even realised he was crying. He put his head in his hands.

The darkness of growing up was evil. It had taken him away from her memories and her away from his life. Peter was alone, once again.

To Grow

By Ciara Walsh Subiran, age 15.

As I grow older I seem
To lose what has happened to me, what I have done,
What I've seen,
Watching as it becomes an almost endless yet startlingly limited
String of memories,
No,
Web of memories,
All jumbled up and confused and missing parts and incomplete
Partially forgotten, yet sparked by most anything.
A picture, a sound,
The blooms of the flowers in spring.
And I struggle to remember, to recall, those little things
How did it feel to be 38 inches tall?
How did it feel to see a world from way, way down?
So very small?
But I imagine,
And I piece together what I can
And I see my small, chubby hand reaching for the giants'
I see the three candles ablaze, flames dancing as I laugh and wait,
As I sit eagerly amidst the celebrations,
Voices chanting in unison, inharmonious and familiar.
And so, remembering, I smile,
And I guess it's okay that I don't remember all the time,
I guess it's fine to imagine
What's been left behind.

The Bird Man

By Maja Malinowska, age15.

It all started with the top hat. One day Mr. Nevara appeared on the street with a top hat sitting on his head. No explanation. Completely out of the blue. People stared, of course, but everyone was too polite to ask. Mr. Nevara was getting old, and with age he became more and more reserved. He barely talked to people, though he was still nice to them; smiling on the street and tilting his antique top hat. He'd let the shopkeeper keep any change, and he gave any leftover food he had to stray animals and birds. He was a gentle soul, no doubt about that, he was just also...distant. I don't think he was close with many people in the village. Unfortunately, the gap only grew wider as time moved on.

As I said, it started with the top hat. He wore it all day, every day. No one knew where he got it from, it just suddenly appeared one day. It was quite strange, but nobody thought much of it; just an old man doing weird things. However, it didn't stop at the top hat.

His next phase came with a cloak. He still wore the top hat; he just added the cloak to it. It was quite a large one too; it covered his whole body, from the neck down, all the way down to his heavy black boots. It looked heavy, yet it seemed swift at the same time, like the movements of a black feathered bird. And he wore this all through the summer's sweltering days. Every day he would go on a walk, and every day he would wear the cloak. By now people started looking strangely at him; children pointed fingers and mothers ushered them quickly away. He was still the nice person he had always been, but people slowly stopped returning that kindness. One by one they dropped out – started talking behind his back. Mr. Nevara either paid no heed to it or was simply oblivious to what was going on around him. Either way, he survived the summer. Sometime during autumn is when people began to genuinely worry about his sanity.

Around October, Mr. Nevara started wearing a gas mask, which covered his whole face. His eyes were just two glass circles, his mouth a filter jutting out. His breathing could be heard before he could be seen. I'm sure he still smiled at everyone he passed by, fed all the stray animals. But by now people thought he was acting ridiculously. Children openly giggled and pointed, their parents didn't stop them anymore; sometimes they would even join in. The older kids would play dares in front of his house. Once they even went as far as throwing a stone through one of his windows; he never got it fixed. By now, nobody liked him anymore; he had become an outcast.

Even so, he went on his daily walks. The cloak seemed to stick to his body, making two awkward wing-like things where his arms were. Not only the arms; his whole body started to resemble that of a bird's. After a while he didn't walk anymore; he waddled, sometimes bouncing down the street. His long spine was bent forwards, making him seem smaller than he actually was. If someone were to compare him to any animal, they'd say he looked like a crow. A human crow.

And so he lived his life as a human crow. He stopped going on walks eventually; just stayed at home all day. Near the end of December the police got reports from a number of the villagers, pleading for them to come and investigate his house. His neighbours stated that they heard weird sounds coming from his house; passers-by sometimes caught a glimpse of a feathered creature through the hole in the broken window. After the police ignored the reports for two weeks, the villagers got impatient and started complaining to them every day. Giving up, the police decided to check it out, positive they'd just find an old man doing whatever it is that old men did. When they arrived at Mr. Nevara's house, they knocked politely on the door. No answer. They tried opening the door. Locked. After discussing it between themselves, the police decided to break in, which wasn't as easy as they had initially thought it would be. They struggled for quite some time, and felt humiliation flush their cheeks. However this was all forgotten as soon as they managed to get the door open. Everyone stood rooted to their spot, not quite sure what to think of the current situation. The house was filled with crows. Real, and alive- they took up the whole space in the house. The police ventured in, and carefully made their way up the stairs, making sure they didn't step on anything.

There they saw him – Mr. Nevara, sitting on his bedroom floor. He sat huddled up, with crows surrounding him. He must have heard the police because as soon as they made their way to the top stair, he looked up, his head turning sharply in their direction. As soon as he saw them he shrieked; the noise sounded very much like a crow's cry. Swiftly Mr.

Nevara got up and ran down the flight of stairs, out through the open door, and into the forest behind his house. All the crows followed him, screeching and clawing at the police on their way out.

Mr. Nevara was never found again. There were, however, witnesses, saying that they sighted him deep in the forest, sitting on a branch of a pine tree. Many others suspected that he had died, and that the people who had supposedly spotted him were only seeking attention. Me? I think he lived. I think he stayed with the crows in the forest. I think that, from the very beginning, all he had wanted was a place in which he could belong.

Buildings

By Ruby Ní Dhubhslaine, age 15.

We are all buildings waiting to be lived in,

Waiting now for someone to come –

And not to take or break,

But to make themselves at home.

To unpack their boxes,

To hang up their pictures,

To stub their toe a million times on the coffee table.

And maybe, just maybe,

When they get used to being there in you

And you get used to them being there in you

You might give them

A key to your

Basement of beautiful secrets.

Ending the war for the Earth

By Eliza-Jane Pearman-Howard, age 14.

Mother Earth is dying. The trees try to help her breathe easier but still she breathes unevenly as their numbers lessen. Her animals huddle close to keep her safe, but they too are growing few. Humans steal her wealth from her body. They strip her of her clothes to reach the jewels she keeps beneath. They cut her to extract the very life blood that runs through her veins. She needs help. She needs this war to end. She asks mankind to stop. She asks them to accept the gifts she gives freely without wanting more but men are too greedy. They accept the gifts and then take even more. But they have taken too much and now Mother Earth cannot give any more but still they take and take. I fear that they will never stop taking. Never be happy with what was given. And if they are never happy, they shall take and take until there is no more to take. But I am certain that if that happens then they will find something else to need and want. And take.

Mother Earth sits on her throne. Or, more accurately, she slumps. Her breathing is ragged, and her expression is clearly pained. General Oak stands before her, informing of the progress in the war against man. It is not going well, as he tells it.

'Huge swathes of trees, good trees, are being cut down every minute. The men, they burn them and chop them, their machines going through them like a caterpillar through a leaf.' Mother Earth shook her head sadly and gazed out the cavern opening. Oak was one of the few trees lucky enough to be born in a protected forest. He had never witnessed the cruelty of men or the wickedness of their inventions. He had barely seen a man before the war began. He was not expecting to become a soldier, let alone lead thousands of his brothers and sisters into battle. No one had expected the war. Most plants thought that the humans would do something. Along with the misunderstood warnings that the wildlife was giving them, the humans received warnings from some of their own kind, the few that cared about their home. Mother Earth knew they were silly and unevolved, but she thought even they would fight against their own extinction. The most any of them had done was about five orbits before when their young tried to make them aware. They ignored it of course. That was nineteen orbits after they celebrated the turn of the century. They were a strange race with short minds. They counted only a brief one hundred orbits as a milestone in time when in reality it was a mere blink, a fraction of a quarter moment. Anyway, it was now twenty-four orbits after the centuries turning and the humans had taken no further action to save themselves, so the environment had to take it into their own limbs. The trees had taken up reluctant arms and the animals had united to form a massive force. They had many good soldiers but very few were designed to fight. Mother Earth had lost enough of her forces and she was tired. So tired. She waved the General's reports and plans away and asked in her clear, quiet voice

'Leave me, will you please?' Immediately the cavern emptied. That was the thing. All of her wards heard her when she said anything. All of them except humans. And she was beginning to grow bored of the novelty of their constant ignorance to their surroundings. Sometimes she wished she could just go to sleep. Just slip into the land of dreams where nothing that happened really mattered and all could be controlled. But if she did, where would her troops be? They didn't know how to fight, and definitely didn't know how to live without her. She wished the war could be over and that the humans would just do as she asked. She felt her eyelids grow heavy and fought to keep her eyes open. After a minute she could resist no longer. Her eyelids fluttered then Mother Earth's vision went dark.

She dreamed of the old days when she herself was young and green. There were no advanced species, so she was alone in her thoughts. The only things she had to talk to were the plants and trees. The bugs and small animals made pleasant company but weren't good if you wanted intelligent conversations. Mother Earth spent most of her time walking through the young forests, enjoying the silence and cleanliness of everything. The only things that threatened her were the larger species, but they respected her presence for the most part and left her alone. She missed these days, when there were no factories or cities. There were barely even bipods. No one felt the need to take more than was given. They just accepted it.

When she awoke there were people in her cavern. Not monkeys or trees. Actual people. A pair of them, standing before her, huddled and uncertain. They looked young, although humans didn't change too much when they matured. There were two of them, a male and a female. They seemed scared and neither of them seemed eager to talk. She looked up at them and examined them in closer detail. They both seemed to look quite similar, she assumed they were both part of the same, if not, very similar, gene pool. They both had the same coloured hair, blondish brown, and short. They were quite different in height, one the size of a low hedge, the other maybe would reach a horse's back. Mother Earth stood up and the male one of them stepped back but the female did not. She looked up at Mother Earth in wonder. Mother Earth continued to examine her. She bowed, something only the proud trees of old did nowadays, and spoke.

'Hi.' She whispered quietly and Mother Earth tilted her head. The male followed this female's lead, dropping to his knees and lowering his head respectfully.

'Why are you here, child?' Mother Earth asked the girl. She seemed to be their leader. The girl looked up at her and frowned.

'We want the war to end and we can't get anyone to listen to us when we ask them to stop fighting.' Mother Earth nodded

'Humans are good at not hearing things.' The girl nodded in agreement,

'Sometimes I think we are a little bit too good'. Mother Earth liked this child, she seemed to understand the problems of her people.

'Stand up' she told her, and she did. 'What is your proposal?'

Rayn was nervous. She had never done anything this important before. She and her brother had only ever protested before actual people. Although Mother Earth was real, so it would seem. Rayn had only heard of her in stories before. Stories that were told to her and her brother, Tom, before they went to bed at night. Rayn had only been six when the war started and even back then she understood it better than most adults. She and her brother both seemed far more aware of the fact that humans were in the wrong, not the trees and wildlife. Personally, she couldn't blame the environment for what it started. But that was in the past and now here she was presenting a proposal to the literal Mother of Everything. It could have been worse, she supposed, at least her brother came with her. But that sentence was a terrifying one

'What is your proposal?'

'I cannot say that all of the humans will stop fighting,' she began, and Mother Earth's face immediately darkened. 'I am not important enough to say that all the people on Earth will immediately stop fighting and hold hands and hug each other,' she added as a brief explanation in case the Mother didn't understand. 'But I can say this, if you want humans to listen to you, you will have to be clear and loud. I will do whatever you need, as will my brother. We will tell everyone we know, and we will make sure everyone knows that we need to stop and that we can't go on.' She sped through this speech and was finished in a second. Mother Earth nodded

'Thank you, children, I appreciate your support, but I fear that nothing will get your governments to listen, nothing will make them see that this cannot continue.' She shook her head sadly and turned away.

'But you might.' It was the boy this time. 'I could drive us into Dublin, I still have my learners permit, I'm sure if the actual Earth Mother appeared in front of the government, they might take a bit of notice. Honestly even seeing you like this is…it's not…I don't like it' he spoke smoothly until the last sentence, stuttering as if not wanting to offend her. Mother Earth smiled down at him

'I understand I'm not looking too good,' she gave a short, sad chuckle. 'I don't know about going to this 'Dublin' of yours. I have never been to a human city before, and I don't exactly blend in.' she was right in that fact. Her green skin alone would have been enough to get her arrested, but along with the flowers grown into her hair and the brown clothes made of what looked like mud, she had no chance of getting through anywhere.

'We can get you a shawl or something to cover your head. And an overcoat or something' the girl looked excited 'then all we have to do is show up to the Dáil and say that the leader of the other side wants to talk to the Taoiseach or something. They'd never give up a chance to be the ones to negotiate a surrender. But of course, you would never accept any surrender other than that of the humans.' She was practically jumping up and down and her brother behind her was barely containing himself.

'What if I was caught?' Mother Earth was still sceptical. 'I'm sure the Irish government would also love to be the ones to capture and detain, possibly even execute, the leader of their enemies.' This seemed to bring them both down a bit but after a second the girl spoke up.

'In all the stories you always have magic powers or something,' she seemed hesitant to finish. 'Can't you just use them?' Mother Earth chuckled.

'I haven't used them in over two hundred orbits. They are a little bit rusty to be honest' she looked down at her hands and flexed her fingers. A subtle green light flickered into existence, surrounding her hands and swirling up her arms 'But it could be arranged'

An hour later they were on the road. Tom was in the driver's seat, the 'L' sign up in the window and his licence in the glove compartment. Rayn was sitting beside him and Mother Earth was in the back. He had never imagined that his sister's idea would have gone so well. He only went to make sure she was safe and to support her. Sure, he cared about the environment and was a tiny bit curious about meeting Mother Earth, but he didn't want to present to her and now here he was driving her up to Dublin so she could talk to the Dáil. Tom hadn't thought that he and his sister, seventeen- and eleven-year olds, could have actually made this much of a difference, even if it was likely they were going to be caught. Looking in the rear-view mirror he could see Mother Earth sitting in the back. The shawl and coat had hidden her strangeness but now she looked like some sort of drug dealer or something. He dreaded the toll and dreaded the bridge and dreaded literally everything. He didn't want to get to Dublin.

Mother Earth sat in the back of the car and watched the road go by. She felt tears prick her eyes as she saw what was a beautiful forest filled with life as it was now, a barren grey wasteland, even the bushes along the middle looked barren. It was so horrible even humans seemed to avoid it. There were no cars on this disgusting concrete desert other than themselves.

'Why build this road?' she asked quietly 'there were other roads, about one hundred years ago, you didn't need concrete or tarmac.' Her voice caught on the word concrete and she cleared her throat. 'Roads are more advanced now' Tom shrugged awkwardly

'Why do you need more advanced roads? They are just roads.' Mother Earth seemed angry and frustrated. She gave an angry sigh and crossed her arms. She looked out the window and didn't move again for some time.

Rayn thought that it was going well. She hadn't expected Mother Earth to trust them so quickly, let alone get in the car and let them drive her to a place she'd never been, to talk to people she'd never met. But it was completely fine and had gone down with barely any problems. Mother Earth completely trusted them and Rayn was not about to let her down. Ryan was going to do anything in her power to make sure that the war would end. And that the war would end in a good way not just everyone dying or the government going back to the exact same way it was before the war started. Then nothing would have changed, and humans would go straight back to taking more than they need.

Mother Earth felt quite insulted by the fact the sun was shining brighter than she had seen in the past year. Now the sun hadn't really communicated since the start of the war and there hadn't been a really nice day for ages. The boy parked up the car on a street and they all got out of his car. The two children seemed to know where they were going, and Mother Earth just followed them. There were a few people giving her strange looks and as she walked, she tapped the girl on the back.

'Why are people looking at me so much?' she asked staring back at an elderly couple who were watching her from across the road.

'You do look kind of weird' the girl replied nodding to the giant overcoat that covered Mother Earth's green body.

'None of my animals would stare at someone for looking different' she shook her head, 'how long till we get to the Dáil?'

'About two minutes,' the boy had clearly been listening to the conversation. He looked back at her and then swept his eyes along the street. 'Sooner we're out of sight, the better,' he seemed uncomfortable and sped up his pace of walking. Mother Earth nodded in agreement, even she could sense the hostility radiating from most of the people on the street. They turned left and suddenly the street seemed to empty. It was like they had walked into a different world. The street was dark, even the sun seemed not to penetrate the shadow cast by the giant building dominating the street. Mother Earth knew they had done work on most important buildings since the war, but this was ridiculous. The cold grey structure towered over the houses either side. The columns had sandbags piled at the bottom and there was a high perimeter fence surrounding the whole thing. The add-ons had made the building look like a prison and the lack of colour hurt Mother Earth's eyes as she looked up at the roof, where machine guns were posted at all four corners.

'As if any plants or animals would dare come into this colourless abyss. It is so plain and dead.' She frowned.

'They still have to defend it just in case,' the boy told her, also watching the guns on the roof, two of which also seemed to be watching them.

'There's also the worry that some of the humans who support you and your cause will attack' the girl announced, marching on towards the entrance, 'you are not entirely without support from the humans, just none of the important people like the Taoiseach or any of the TDs support you.'

'Well there used to be an entire party, but they got shut down just after the war started,' the boy shrugged, 'no need for an environmental party when we're fighting the environment,' he said this in a higher tone than usual, as if he had heard it before.

'Who goes there?' the guard had finally noticed them, 'what is your business here?'

Harry was nervous. He imagined that the three people approaching him could hear it in his voice. He had tried to make himself sound as tough as possible, but he always tried to do that among his friends and it always failed there so he assumed it would fail here as well. The group approaching looked quite strange and Harry had hoped they would just back away when he called out, that's what most groups did. Nobody wanted anything to do with the Dáil anymore. To be honest neither did he, he couldn't understand why the stuffy TDs inside the grey prison didn't seem to know that what they were sending thousands of Irish men and women to die for, was wrong. He understood the environment and he had his education cut short because of the need for young boys in the army. None of the people in assembly had, they had had a full and expensive education, and they seemed to find it perfectly alright to keep taking from the Earth forever. People were dying and they were discussing how to send more people over. Harry's brother was dying, and they were discussing how to send Harry to join him. Harry shuddered as he thought about the report his mother had received about the attack. A couple of poison-dart frogs got into the camp. Almost fifty men were poisoned before the alarm was even raised. It resulted, so far, in twenty deaths and a lot of the other men poisoned were still in critical condition in hospital,

Alex being one of them. And now Harry was here when he should be with him. And that group were still coming towards him.

The girl led the way, approaching the soldier on duty. She didn't stop until she was virtually toe to toe with him, which amused Mother Earth as this 'little girl' came up to the soldier's chest. Her brother pulled her back and yanked her behind him, which was slightly better as he was only an inch or two shorter than the guard.

'What is your business?' the man asked again, and Mother Earth replied,

'We have come to talk to the men in charge.'

'The Dáil,' the boy whispered in her ear.

'The Dáil.' She declared. The soldier frowned,

'They are in a meeting right now but if you schedule an appointment with your local TD and then talk to them, they might bring what you want to say to the rest of the TDs.' He seemed nervous and fiddled with the straps on his uniform. He had a rifle strung across his back, but Mother Earth was willing to bet her life he wouldn't use it. What the soldier said seemed to anger the girl and she stuck out her tongue at him.

'Do you not think we have already tried that!' she was growing angrier and angrier and Mother Earth could see her face growing redder and redder. Mother Earth decided it was time to interrupt, before the girl strangled the guard to death.

'I do not make 'appointments" she told him and threw back her shawl and tossed it and her coat to the side, 'I find showing up in the moment helps with a lot of things.' The machine guns on the roof were instantly pointing at her and the guard they had been talking to stumbled backwards and fumbled around with the strap on his rifle, trying to get it to turn around. After a minute he managed to get it turned around and he pointed it at Mother Earth and shouted,

'Surrender yourself.' The barrel was shaking and the man at the trigger was visibly sweating. In this new position something jogged Mother Earth's memory.

'You look familiar,' she told him, tilting her head back and forth.

'I've never seen you before in my life' the boy stammered. He looked more like a boy now, shaking and nervous.

'Do you have a brother?' she asked quietly, and the boy gasped and nodded his head slowly. 'I walked into that camp' Mother Earth remembered that night, 'the frogs had not meant to cause the damage they did. The entire camp was in bits. I came to see if I could help, maybe save some of them, usually I can but this time I couldn't. The camp was completely unguarded, everyone was too busy with themselves, rolling around and screaming. Except one. A man stood before me and raised his gun. I could see that he too had been affected as he was sweating profusely. He shook and I could see the pain in his eyes. I told him he should not be on his feet as it spreads the poison quicker, but he shook his head and said he had to protect his friends. I tried to help him, but he would not let me near. Eventually I left.' Mother Earth frowned and shook her head sadly. The boy standing before them let go of his gun. It swung down on the strap that held it to him and dangled in the air just above the ground. The boy started to cry. The girl rushed to him and wrapped her arms around his waist,

'It's okay' she whispered, and he sniffled. The girl's brother frowned but the boy stood up and turned around. He waved at the machine guns and three of them turned away.

'My name's Harry' he told them. Mother Earth was not in the habit of exchanging names, but she did realize it was a human custom.

'I'm Mother Earth and these are my companions...' she also realized she didn't know either of the children's names.

'I'm Tom and this is my sister Rayn' the brother told the soldier quickly and they were all introduced.

'So, can we talk to the Dáil now?' Mother Earth asked and Harry nodded his head,

'Provided they let you in, what are you here for, anyway?' Harry asked raising an eyebrow, he seemed to have a distressing thought. 'You aren't surrendering, are you?' this idea seemed to worry him, 'please don't, if you do things will go back to the way they were before, and Alex will have suffered for nothing'

'Alex?' Mother Earth enquired.

'My brother,' Harry paused for a moment before looking up, 'everyone knows deep down you are right in what you do anyway, except the Taoiseach and all the TDs and important people.' This was said quickly, but Mother Earth shook her head

'I will not surrender, I am here about discussing your people and country's surrender.' This seemed to please Harry and he turned and walked towards the domineering structure.

'Come on,' he called back to them and the three followed hesitantly. It took a minute for them to get inside the building but when they did, they saw a ridiculous sight. On the inside the place that looked like a prison looked like a castle. It was all carpeted in red, the polished wood adding to the expensive posh home design style. Harry went off and after a minute returned with a silly looking man in a grey suit and blue tie. The man said, 'Come with me please,' before walking off. If the stares had been bad on the street, in here they were like lasers. It felt like hundreds of red-hot beams were glaring into Mother Earth's general body. It felt good to be out of the coat and shawl. She was not used to having to cover up her natural differences to the humans. The man they were following led them into a large room lined with chairs and told them 'go in when you hear somebody call for you.' Then he left and they were alone again. Harry sat down on one of the waiting chairs and Tom followed quickly, lying across three chairs and closing his eyes. Rayn sat down on the floor, despite the lines of chairs left and after a moment Mother Earth sat down beside her, taking a cushion off one of the chairs and plonking it down on the floor to sit on. Rayn didn't take a cushion and Mother Earth watched as the child removed, first her shoes, and then her socks, wiggling her feet into the red carpet and stroking her hands up and down along it as well. Mother Earth had no shoes to remove but as she moved her foot along the carpet it did feel good, like moss on the floor of a clearing in a wood. After about two minutes a voice called 'enter' and the group rose to their feet. Harry opened the door for them, and Mother Earth led the way into the massive meeting room of the Irish government.

Tom was terrified. They were actually here. How did this happen? Why were they in the Dáil? And what's more, why was the Dáil letting them in?

It was absurd. And now he, and his sister were standing in front of north of one hundred and fifty TDs and senators. And the Taoiseach. What was he doing? This wasn't nearly as easy as he'd imagined. Even after they got Mother Earth to agree, he assumed they'd be turned away at the door, but no. But he had to do this now. Even if he could leave, he knew his sister wouldn't, especially not when they were this close to ending everything. No, they would never get this opportunity again, possibly no one would ever, and they couldn't, no he couldn't let down the entire world. What would dad say?

Mother Earth stood before the Irish government. They surrounded her, the seats curving round in an oval with her and her group standing in the middle. These men and women had been chosen to represent the Irish people. Mother Earth was literally talking to the puppeteers of Ireland.

'Hello,' she began, assuming that politeness was the way to go, considering what she was about to propose, 'thank you for agreeing to meet with me.'

'Cut the niceties and tell us what you want' this came from a smug man standing in a box, facing the rest of the people in the room.

'And who would you be?' Mother Earth was confused. She did not come here to be shouted at by some man in a box.

'I am the Taoiseach' the man addressed her, looking down at her from his position above them all. 'Oh, that's nice.' She smiled at him, her voice dripping in sarcasm 'I am Mother Earth and I am here to tell you to stop.' The low murmurs and conversations that had been going on since her entry all stopped. Even the smug man in his box looked shocked. 'You have taken too much, I cannot supply what you want any longer.' She had the entire room's attention 'surrender yourselves or I will be forced to do something I will regret. I raised you since you were mere single celled organisms and I always helped when you needed, I sheltered you from disaster, thinking one day you might grow to be my helpers, worthy of having my constant attention. I loved you. But now, I want to still care for you, but I cannot.' The silence in the room was almost deafening. The only sound was the ticking of the clock on the wall.

I'm not sure of how to end this. I think that is because it has two endings, the good and the bad.

The good, the Dáil listens to Mother Earth and stops. They withdraw their troops and ban any products harmful to the environment. Harry's brother, Alex, comes home, Mother Earth heals him, and they live happily ever after. Rayn and Tom grow up and move around a lot, trying to keep all the world safe from climate change and everything else. Basically, everyone lives happily ever after.

The bad, the Dáil doesn't listen to Mother Earth. They keep fighting and keep taking and polluting. Harry's brother dies along with millions or possibly billions of other soldiers. The war goes on till neither side can fight anymore. Rayn and Tom are both killed when they try to talk to a different country and the government building collapses in an attack, killing everyone inside. Climate changes continues and after a few years, greenhouse gases block out the sun and everyone who wasn't killed in the war, dies anyway. Everyone dies forever after.

I don't know, but maybe you can help me decide. We could make all the difference. Stop using plastic, stop buying palm oil, use solar or wind power. Basically, use everything the Earth intended us to use, no more. Now I'm not going to put in a solid ending to this story. The choice is yours. And to all who think this is a story, it's not, it's the future, just with added fantasy elements. I know which ending I'd choose. So, please. Choose wisely.

Goodbye

The Night Walk

By Tara Finnegan, age 15.

'Just keep walking,' I kept repeating in my head over and over again. This was a sentence I had told myself countless times to try and calm myself down. Yet it made no difference as I would always still panic. I was a very anxious person so this type of situation was not unusual for me. It was a bitter December night. There was a cool wind blowing around me furiously, making my skin feel as cold as ice. I was walking home from my friend's house, alone. She wanted to walk me halfway, but I told her she should just stay home and that I would be fine on my own. Little did I know that was my first mistake. I wasn't even that far from my house, maybe about ten minutes if I walked at a quick pace. It was only about ten past seven in the evening yet there was still complete darkness outside. The only light was the street lamps trying their hardest to illuminate the roads, but they made very little difference. I lived in a small town with a low population. It wasn't near any cities and we were mainly surrounded by huge fields. It was one of those towns where everyone knew each other and nothing bad ever really happened. I knew it was a safe town, but I still couldn't stop my mind from thinking things I wish it didn't. Like I said, I was a very anxious person, so I never really felt one hundred percent safe. I lived my life with a constant fear in the back of mind. Questions like 'what if this happens?' and 'am I safe?' tortured me day after day. They followed me wherever I went and never let me rest. I tried my best to not let these thoughts have any control over me. I tried to push them back to the deepest and darkest place in my mind in the hope that they would not surface yet they still seemed to ring in my head like deafening alarms in many situations, especially situations like this. The situation I was in was that I was walking alone in the dark. I would not say that I was afraid of the dark, but I still didn't like walking alone in it with only my torturous thoughts to keep me company. My imagination used the darkness surrounding me to create ways to scare me.

I put on my earphones to try and drown out my thoughts. This was my usual move. I found it comforting to just listen to music and focus on the lyrics. It usually distracted me. But that night was different. Something just felt wrong. The music had a different effect on me. Instead of comforting and distracting me like it usually did, it made things worse. The noises in the songs had convinced me that there were noises happening around me and I didn't like not being able to hear my surroundings as I felt like one of those movie characters with an impending doom nearing them yet they're so terrifyingly unaware of their fate. I liked being aware of what was happening all around me, it gave me a sort of calmness. I decided to take my earphones out of my ears and start walking at a quicker pace. 'Just five minutes until I'm home,' I reassured myself.

I'm not sure when I started being such an anxious person. I was so carefree as a child, but as I grew older I started worrying more and more. I guess that's what happens to us all. When we're kids we don't realise what dangers the world holds and what can happen to us, yet as we grow older reality sinks in and we begin to see the world for what it really is, our worst nightmare.

I was still walking alone. I kept looking behind me to check if there was anybody to be seen. I couldn't see anyone. I felt like I was walking down a never ending road, all alone. But that's when I saw it. My whole body stopped. It felt as though the world around me just paused. I didn't blink. I didn't move. I didn't breathe. I couldn't believe what I was seeing. I had been so focused on my thoughts that I hadn't actually looked down at the ground until now. I looked down and saw my shadow. This itself didn't scare me. What scared me was that my shadow wasn't the only one there. There was a much taller shadow beside mine, as if there was someone tall walking beside me, yet there was nobody around me. Without giving myself any time to process, I just started running. I didn't even know why I was running or what was happening but I just continued to run, because I was scared of what might happen if I didn't. I ran as fast as I physically could.

With shaky breaths and a racing heartbeat, I turned the corner onto a field. That was my second mistake. The field seemed to be even darker than the road before it yet I didn't care. I just kept running. I knew that once I got past this field I would be home. I was just worried that I wouldn't get past this field. I was too scared to even dare look behind me because I knew that what I saw would just make me even more terrified than I already was. I had always been happy in the past when I looked behind me and saw nobody, yet this time I knew that seeing nobody would just make it worse, because then it would mean that it was actually a shadow I was running from. There was an old legend my nan used to tell me as a child.

It was called 'the shadow woman'. It was about a woman named Marie. She was murdered in our town on the 9th of December 1907. She was walking in the dark one night alone and all of a sudden a man came out from the shadows and stabbed her to death. They say that her spirit never left the town and that she lives in the shadows and terrorizes people that are vulnerable as a way of getting revenge because nobody helped her when she was being killed. Some people say they have even seen her, but a lot of people say that she's in the form of a shadow. A dark shadow always following you and seeming to be watching you. I never believed that story and regarded it as something adults tell children to scare them to get them to come home before it gets dark out. Yet in that moment something just seemed so real about that story and seeing that shadow in my vulnerable state just convinced me it was true. I had a gut feeling that I just wasn't alone and that there was a presence with me, a presence in the form of pure evil.

I was still running through the field. It felt as though I had been running for so long, yet I wasn't going anywhere. I could still see the huge distance between me and safety. My running came to a sudden halt when my leg got caught in a branch lying on the ground. I frantically tried to get loose. I could practically feel my heart banging against my chest. I couldn't stop shaking. I couldn't seem to get free. I felt trapped. I was hyperventilating. I couldn't concentrate. I wasn't thinking straight. It felt as though I was moving at a hundred miles per hour yet I was standing still. Millions of thoughts were running around in my head. I started to lose focus and everything became blurry. Black started seeping in through the sides of my eyelids and suddenly my body hit the cold ground.

All The Lonely People

By Ella O'Rourke, age 15.

> 'All the lonely people, where do they all come from?
> All the lonely people, where do they all belong?'
>
> - The Beatles, Eleanor Rigby

Nadia's grubby scarred hands push the levers into gear and she checks all the levels; the spacecraft churns into motion. Here she goes. The thing she's wanted to do ever since she was old enough to understand the news (younger than average) is go to space, but not for the reason you'd assume. She starting drawing up blueprints for her own spaceship – The Contingency –- when she was ten and she knew even then that she would succeed, because she needed to. Her aspiration to become an astronaut began when she found out about climate change and how quickly humans were destroying the Earth. She was horrified at the prospect of living on a dead pulp floating through the abyss, so decided to take it into her own hands to journey into the abyss and toward a living Something Else. Of course she gave her family and friends the chance to go with her, because she knew it would be a happier way of living (don't ask how she knew this – it was her intuition which was usually pretty spot on), but they fully declined the offer and quite frankly, they thought she was crazy to want to risk her life in order to save it. Now you see where they were coming from.

...

Nadia persisted with her spacecraft plans and ended up with a PhD in engineering and aeronautics along with a master's degree in mathematics and physics. Her determination was guaranteed to hold to her in space.

Nadia Goldstein was always an ambitious child; her parents used to find her doodles and scribbles of her dreams scattered all over the house. She hardly ever asked them for money – she worked for all of her desires by herself, it was her nature. So the fact that she's now being launched into space by her own spacecraft isn't much of a surprise, really.

She's always spent as much of her time as possible alone because of how others treat her, which has had its toll on her mental wellbeing but has simultaneously prepared her for spending the rest of her life in potential — potential – isolation.

Her time and work are reflected on her exterior: her blue and green shoulder length hair (which she dyed to resemble what she wished Earth still looked like) is frayed; her eyes are misty blue-grey, clouded; she's marked all over with cuts and scrapes, stained with oil; she has calloused fingertips and dry fragile lips, which she gnaws on now in concentration.

...

The craft forces her back as it plummets faster forward, her breath catches and Nadia is finally hit with the fear she's been expected to feel her whole life; she could swear The Contingency is being fuelled by adrenaline in this moment. But there's no going back now, not after spending her whole life getting ready for this moment and everything that lies ahead of it. She can't let herself return to the dying Earth when she's dreamt for years about leaving it. The Contingency is vertical, she can feel gravity telling her off, and she's gleeful, she's finally doing it, she's done it, she's left the atmosphere! With no one here to cheer for her, she laughs to herself. This could go terribly or excellently, but she is in control of how she looks at it. Nadia Goldstein has reached space. Now she has to find her landing ground.

...

Her initial plan was Mars because that's all the astronomers ever talk about, life form, life form life form life form. But from the very beginning Nadia was gathering supplies for every possible and impossible situation that the universe could throw at her, so she then began considering Europa, a moon of Jupiter. Pretty quickly that became her number one destination — its atmosphere consists solely of oxygen and it has a water-ice crust which she has created a machine for extracting oxygen from to refill her tanks with.

...

She spends a few years gazing in wonder at the Milky Way passing her window and thinking about how she did this whole thing by herself. She grows fond of her vacuum-packed ready meals. After a while she spots the silver-bronze shimmering sphere that is Europa, and steers The Contingency toward it.

Nadia lands softly on the smooth surface of the moon. She hooks herself up to her first tank (although the atmosphere here consists solely of O_2, she still needs to breathe in nitrogen, carbon dioxide, and a tiny amount of argon) and opens the hatch. She's done it, she's on Europa! The astronaut steps out onto the surface and feels free, free from judgement, free from responsibility, free from the idiots and bullies.

...

The dense silence begins to thin, which surprises Nadia, but her curious side leaps out like a wild cat and she looks around, alert. There's a very faint high-pitched hum coming from seemingly all around her, a sound she's never heard before, a sound that soothes her despite its unfamiliarity. A glowing something comes into her peripheral vision. It floats toward her and halts at eye level. It's an orb the size of a cricket ball, bright as a star, ice blue glowing white, burning against itself into the space around it. It holds Nadia's gaze tightly. She's enraptured. The energy it gives off is calm and friendly. After a few moments, it speaks to her – there is no sound, she just feels the words: I knew your arrival was inevitable.

...

Nadia is confused, but something about the orb won't allow her to panic (although Nadia's never been much of a panicker). 'How did you know?' she asks. The orb hovers for a second and then moves away from her, leading her forward. She walks after it, intrigued. The surface of Europa is smooth and the silver and bronze silicate rock seems to swirl beneath her feet. The air is still. As she follows the orb further into the unknown, she smells mint. Lime. Raspberry. Orange. The mint is the strongest, tickling her nose hairs. The orb leads her to the smells and what comes into view confuses her even more about what the orb said; a vast plane of clusters and clusters of tiny, tiny plants, mostly mint, but some fruits and vegetables. Some clusters are bigger than others and more spaced out, and each is in a different formation. Nadia surveys the sight for a moment and the realisation hits her – this is a map of Earth! Each cluster of plants represents a country and each little plant represents a person! Her thoughts of incredulity and wonder are interrupted by the second wave of words from the orb: Represents or is?

...

Nadia looks to her left where the orb is now. It can read her mind? She's certain she didn't say any of that out loud.

I can read all minds. I control them if I like.

'Should I be afraid of you? I can leave right now if I want to, you know.' Nadia goes to step back, but at the last second decides she doesn't need to. Yes, that was her own conscious decision. Oh no.

The orb doesn't answer her question. This is indeed a map of your origin planet Earth, and each plant is a person – it does not merely represent one as you suggested. What makes each plant a person is the fact that if it were just a representation, I could only monitor its actions and I would have no control. But I make elaborate plans and instructions for each one to follow over the course of its lifetime and ensure it follows those instructions and carries out the plan on Earth.

...

Nadia takes a moment to process this. She lets the hum of the orb wash over her. Is she in danger?

You're not in any danger.

'Stop reading my mind! And telling me I'm not in any danger is exactly the kind of thing you would say if I was in an unfathomable amount of danger!' she snaps. She feels the orb giggle. Hang on, did the orb just giggle?

Maybe.

'Stop that! I was going to ask: what is your so-called 'plan' for Earth?'

A beat – the orb is hesitant.

It's a long story, but I know you have your whole life to listen, so here goes.

...

Nadia sits cross-legged and listens to – well, feels – the orb talk for what feels like minutes, but probably takes an hour or two (not that Earth time means anything here). It tells of how the Orbs began; a fragment of the iron-nickel core of Europa broke away and split into two parts, one made its way to Earth and one lived here on its own moon. The Earth Orb never came back home but kept in contact with the Europa Orb through their magnetic signals. The Earth Orb would report regularly to its twin about the developments of the planet; the dinosaurs, the first people, the first civilisations. When climate change began, the Earth Orb was mildly concerned but the Europa Orb was terrified - it knew what would happen to the humans' planet, and for some reason it wanted to save them. Shortly after the humans began their self-destruct, the Earth Orb imploded.

...

The Europa Orb lost their connection and knew it had ended; the Orb had never been lonely before, it had always had a companion to communicate with, even though it had this moon to itself. It set out on a mission to save the humans by itself. Some years later, it felt somewhat defeated, but had begun to care about the creatures even more, so knew it couldn't give up on saving them from themselves. The Orb became obsessed with controlling them, steering their mint leaves in all sorts of different directions, until it realised that what it had been trying to do was not distract itself from the loss of its twin, not save the humans from their impending doom, but to direct them towards Europa. All it wanted was someone to be with it on its ice rock. So it found a baby — the first human had to be moulded from birth, more intelligent than the rest, must have the Orb's own fear instilled rigidly, must realise how dangerous their habitat planet was as soon as possible to really persist with the journey - and it began instructing, carefully choosing the kinds of people who interacted with her, how they affected her, what her parents and teachers thought of her plans to leave. The Orb made sure she was lonely. And now, here she was. Nadia Goldstein, the first human to travel to Europa. The first human to never leave.

...

Nadia is dumbstruck. None of her dreams were made by her, none of the people she talked to were meant to like her, none of the teachers she hated were supposed to be likeable, she didn't just have 'good intuition'; it was all in this plan that some orb made.

She felt the Orb clear its non-existent throat pointedly. I am not 'some orb'.

'I'm trying to have a moment here!'

...

Over the next few decades, Nadia and the Orb bonded and became each other's everything – human beings still had to be controlled from Europa because the moment the Earth Orb had entered Earth's atmosphere, the planet and moon had become co-dependent, so now the plants could not be neglected just because the Europa Orb had gained a friend. Nadia enjoyed nurturing the plants and every now and then she would have to destroy one, but that was okay too. Someone had to do it.

Her green and blue faded from her hair; it returned to its natural ash blonde and grew past her waist. Her misty blue-greys became clearer and brighter despite her fatigue; the workload was constant as the Orb didn't need sleep, so Nadia had to adapt. Her hands became softer through caring for the plants.

Nadia and the Orb lived together in harmony. More and more humans travelled to Europa led by the Goldsteins who missed Nadia too much so wished to spend their last years with her on a foreign moon than without her on a familiar planet. Eventually, the entire human race lived on Europa – the plants disappeared and the Orb was content. Human beings apparently aged significantly slower on Europa, so Nadia got to see the plan succeed.

...

But one day, the Orb's signals became weaker and its hum, that ever-present hum that Nadia had grown accustomed to, became quieter and quieter. The white glow that surrounded it grew dimmer. The last thing

Nadia felt it say was: The humans give off an energy only humans can process… I think the humans were the thing that killed my twin. I now know what it felt - the things your people keep inside wear away the creatures around you, and we Orbs cannot develop anything in return, we merely take it in and cannot do anything to dispose of it. We crave your energy but it eats us up. I must leave, Nadia. Maybe you'll still hear me.

...

And with that, the Orb floated away from Nadia. She was heaving, sobbing, weeping, no, it couldn't be leaving, it couldn't be, but when she saw the tiny supernova that was its implosion, she felt herself loosen. She wasn't being controlled anymore, her mind wasn't being stretched or pulled anymore. She was thinking her own thoughts for the first time in her entire life at the age of fifty. Nadia was lonely now, but she was free.

The Daughter That Never Was

By Eva Osborne, age 17.

She spoke of it last night.

The fire was down to its last dying embers.

She was humming to herself as she crocheted,

While he watched the news with just enough interest to keep himself awake.

The silence was nothing new.

This was what the spontaneous outings and passionate lust became when it was committed to,

And both were happy with this commitment.

But, for her,

Something would always be missing.

Two boys, three years apart.

The eldest was a scholar,

He called him the next Einstein.

The youngest was a troublemaker,

He reminded her of herself as a child.

They loved them so wholly, so intensely.

They loved them through and through.

She had never seen a man look at something with such love and pride in his eyes.

They stopped after that.

They didn't want to, but she couldn't carry anymore.

She would always long for the daughter that never was.

She brings her crocheting to a pause to break the silence.

'If we had a daughter...'

She didn't know where to go with it.

He didn't give her much time to decide.

'It's a bit late for this.'

That upset her.

She didn't let it faze her though, this Kerry woman could never be silenced and he loved her for it.

'She would've had Kerry roots...well, and English ones. But she'd have Kerry blood. She would've been absolutely stunning- red hair, brown eyes. She would've been gorgeous, smart and fair. My brains, your brawn. She'd have gotten the best grades in her year, no doubt. Mature, but not cold. Fun, but not naive...'

Her eyes were filling with tears.

He knew she could go on and she did too.

But it was late,

And the fire was out.

He looked at her, his tired blue eyes reflected the television screen.

'I think it's time for bed dear.'

The Waiting Game

By Leah Farrell, age 17.

Wanderlust. That infectious feeling of wanting to explore every corner, every nook and cranny of the world around you. That infectious feeling of falling in love with somewhere new and never waiting to leave. This place is no different. Twenty-four hours. Only twenty-four hours to soak up every ounce of personality this city exudes before my connecting flight home. I'm not about to waste it.

Looking out the foggy window to a dewy New York City, it's impossible not to feel in awe. Building after building passes in a blur as we near my bus stop. I pull the worn, bobbly sleeve of my knit jumper over my fist and wipe it across the cool glass. I crane my neck. Buildings of all dimensions, short or tall, wide or narrow, rise from the earth around me, like mountains made of glass and concrete, reaching for the sky. Some succeed, their tops invisible, engulfed by the seemingly calm grey clouds shimmering against the backdrop of a royal blue sky. Shades of red and orange run throughout, as if painted on with a single smooth brush stroke and the sun rises shyly from its perch behind a tall skyscraper, its rays softening the city's streets.

We come to a halt. My body straining against the frayed seat belt for a moment before relaxing. I check my watch. 6:57am. Rush hour in New York City. The endless array of traffic backed up the length of the avenue moves at a snail's pace and I startle in my seat as the piercing sound of car horns reverberates relentlessly. All part of the New York City experience, I tell myself.

The man sitting across from me fidgets in his seat, his head scanning the reality of the surrounding traffic jam. His eyebrows knit together, and his noses scrunches up in irritation – not in an unattractive way I must admit. He turns his head slightly and I notice a small nick across his jaw, as if he cut himself shaving. He's dressed immaculately, his charcoal-grey suit tailored and pressed to perfection. With certain movements, I can see his silver engraved cufflinks glint in the sunlight before disappearing again under the sleeve of his suit jacket. The 'click, click' from the heel of his polished leather shoe hitting the grubby bus floor does nothing to hide his impatience and as I settle back into my seat, I can't help but wonder why a man like him would be riding the bus in the first place.

After what feels like an eternity, the bus manoeuvres into my stop with a deflated sigh. Stepping out onto the cracked concrete path, the thrill of exploring the streets of Manhattan hits me. The sun sits proudly for all to see by now, but I can't escape the chill in the air as I pass through a bustling intersection.

Skilfully dodging an unsuspecting coffee cup in my path, I can feel myself salivating as the strong aroma of freshly brewed black coffee reaches my nostrils and I can almost hear the hot liquid sloshing inside the plastic cup as the hand gripping that oh-so-essential caffeine boost rushes by. My stomach rumbles loudly, pleading with me and I've no intention of ignoring it.

My sights are set on one thing and one thing only. Breakfast. A never-ending stack of thick, fluffy American pancakes drowning in a sea of golden maple syrup and a layer of freshly whipped cream piled generously on top... or maybe a big plate of warm waffles, crisp on the outside yet airy on the inside. The square pats of butter soaking into the dough and melting slowly, turning from a solid into a liquid against the heat and trickling softly into the practical compartments – existing solely to catch the syrupy butter and juicy berries sprinkled on top. How would I ever decide?

A long metal subway car sits on the street in front of me, as if someone had just picked it up and placed it there at random. Renovated with vibrant red and yellow panels along the bottom and loud neon letters spelling 'DINER' above the door, they're definitely not going for 'inconspicuous'. Pulling open the stiff door, the scent of smoky rashers sizzling on a hot plate and bitter coffee almost slaps me in the face and the air feels thick with grease. People sit on glossy red leather bar stools or in booths, either chatting to the waitresses topping up coffee mugs with a certain prowess or hunched over this morning's paper.

The ambiance is electric, the constant chatter ringing in my ears as I sink into a booth next to the front window. Through the excitement, The Bee Gees play from an old jukebox.

'Listen to the ground... There is movement all around... There is something goin' down... And I can feel it'. Tapping my foot to the catchy beat, I barely register the waitress sashaying towards me. 'Coffee?' she enquires chirpily, flashing a perfect red lipstick-stained smile as she leans down to fill my large coffee mug, slightly over-ambitious as a trail of the liquid runs down the side before plopping onto the metal table.

'What can I get ya?' Her voice sweet and thick with a distinctive New York accent.

'I'll take the stack of three pancakes.'

'And a side? Bacon? Eggs? We do hard scrambled, soft scrambled, sunny side up, over easy, poached, hard boiled, soft boiled or an omelette.' I blink. Her words all running into each other, so much so that it sounds like a whole different language.

She stands waiting, hip cocked, head tilted, that zealous smile still plastered to her petite face. 'Bacon...' I reply hesitantly. Surely that's the safest option here.

'Great. And bread with that? We have rye, whole wheat, white, brown, sourdough, soda, baguettes, bagels, brioche – '.

'No bread!' I interrupt, almost out of breath myself.

'Stack of three pancakes and a side of bacon coming right up!' She turns on her heel and I gulp down my coffee like a madwoman, wincing as it hits my tongue and sets my throat aflame.

Feeling the tension leave my body, I glace at my watch. 8:32am. The day's only beginning. Reaching across the table, I grab a battered copy of today's New York Post. I smooth it out but the stubborn, well-read pages curl in on themselves, the edges dog eared. 'Top Designers Will Junk Punk, You'll See Softer Looks This Spring' reads a bold headline, the curly font standing out ostentatiously in the midst of column after column of modest Times New Roman.

In an attempt to occupy myself as I wait, I rest my head in my hands and start reading. Out of the corner of my eye, I spot a perky waitress saunter towards me, carrying plates up the length of her arms with practised ease. I sit up, tossing the paper to one side, ready to give those pancakes pride of place. My salivary glands start working in desperate anticipation, but my heart sinks as she moves to serve the table behind me. Cruel.

Looking out the window, I distract myself by observing the throngs of people passing by. A woman catches my attention, stumbling as she moves frantically, knocking against everyone in her path. On the opposite side of the street, a young couple does the same and I'm about to put it down to poor punctuality until almost simultaneously, people start loading out of their cars, abandoning them, not even sparing a glance to close the doors.

A shiver runs down my spine and the hairs on my arms stand on edge. The same expression visible on each and every face in front of me. Eyes wide, like a deer caught in the headlights. Mouth hanging open. Shock. Disbelief. Fear. Things they all have in common right in this moment. I see lips moving. Panicked. Tear-stained cheeks. Violent sobs rocking children's bodies, threatening to shatter their bones like glass. Parents whispering words of reassurance, trying to hold it together, but none succeeding.

Sirens. Everything around me drowned out as the sirens wail like a baby in distress with no one to comfort it. My heart jumps wildly in my chest. Each thump audible in my own ears as I stay frozen, my chipped finger nails digging into the cold, smooth leather beneath me. Too terrified to move. Too terrified of what disaster is waiting for me only steps away.

'Chak-chak-chak-chak-chak'. The steady rhythm of helicopter blades beat overhead. Before I realise what I'm doing, I yank open the door to the diner, leaving any sense of safety I have behind. I follow everyone's gaze. My stomach lurching and twisting, my breath knocked from my body and I fight to get enough oxygen into my lungs like an old man after a lifetime of smoking.

I shuffle forward on unsteady legs, my whole body suddenly weak, my knees locking with each step, protesting. Sweat prickles on the surface of my skin yet I feel chills travelling from my feet to my fingertips.

Two towers stand side by side in solidarity above the New York City skyline. Streams of thick black smoke billow from gaping wounds on the sides of each tower, their paths intertwining against the force of the wind, an attempt at a final embrace. As I look on, the South Tower crumbles, collapsing in on itself in defeat and filling the atmosphere with ash and debris. All those lives. Lost. Now we play the waiting game. It's only a matter of time before the second tower joins the first.

Dignity

By Deirdre Hamill, age 16.

The length of my hair does not make discrimination fair.

The colour of my skin cannot help prejudice win.

The style of my clothes is not a prison that determines my sexuality.

I should be able to stand tall and free, release myself from the strings that hold me

Captive from humanity's acceptance and equality.

But I will fly like a bird,

High and happily.

I will overlook the negativity and I will feed on empathy.

I will strive to see the positivity.

And my wings will not fail me or be shot down by bigotry.

I am a person and always will be,

If you cannot see that, where is your dignity?

A Civilian's Rising

By Philippa Byford, age 17.

Monday 24th of April dawned like any other that year, bright and clear with a gentle breeze off the Liffey waters. Light streamed in through the shop window, illuminating the floor timbers in its soft, golden shine. As was customary, Diarmuid O'Rourke had propped that window open, just as he did every morning he could, letting the smell of warm bread out onto the quayside and allowing the soft echoes of lapping water into the shop. Nestled in the shadow of Liberty Hall, Diarmuid had grown fond of the mornings, rising each time with Dublin's waking stirs.

As the loaves rose in the ovens, he flicked though that morning's newspaper; once more, the words 'Sinn Fein Rising!' seemed splattered over every page. They'd lost their effect on Diarmuid by now, no longer exciting him with the ideas of revolution. He'd lost track of whether a rising would ever actually happen in Ireland, or even if MacNeill would make up his mind.

But never mind, he thought, folding the paper away and watching his little Rachel dance around the shop, showing off her new bottlecap necklace. She'd managed to string them all together, somehow, with a length of string and was already in the process of making another, smaller one, for her dolly. A smile; he couldn't help it.

Diarmuid was just setting a fresh loaf on the counter when the bell over the door chimed. He looked up, smiling as he always did at the sound. 'Mrs Doherty, good morning! The usual?'

'They have the GPO,' she blurted out, chasing her breath. Diarmuid smiled on.

'I know. I heard that little fellow reading out his wares on the steps when I was delivering Mr Quinn's daily bread. A funny little stunt, really.'

'I heard they took Boland's and the Four Courts too!'

Ah, Mondays. He reached for a fresh, brown loaf and a sheet of paper, recalling the deep green flag they'd raised as he'd come back to the shop.

'Now, Mrs Doherty, calm yourself. It'll likely blow over by the time your husband comes home. No fear in that.'

'But they have-!' A nervous glance to where Rachel was playing with her dolly. 'They have guns,' she hissed over the counter. 'I saw Ciara Flanagan's boy outside the GPO with one! Guns, Diarmuid. It's not right, not right at all.'

Diarmuid smiled, but she was right. Just the other week, Dónal Flanagan had been standing just there, a grin stretched over his cheeky little face as he bought some penny sweets.

Fifteen was far too young to be switching toffees for bullets.

'I'm sure it'll all be fine,' he said, handing over the wrapped loaf. 'You'll see.'

She eyed him sceptically and he smiled again.

'We'll talk to you.'

And with that, she was gone, the chiming bell, missing loaf and a few pennies the only evidence she'd ever even been.

But as Wednesday rolled around, seemingly a century later, Ireland proved Diarmuid wrong. The sounds of war, of shouting and gunfire and screaming became background noise, replacing the squawking seagulls that had been the city's music when Diarmuid had first returned to Dublin.

'Is everyone all right?' he called, peering out from behind the counter at the refugees gathered in his shop. Some were hiding under his little display table, which they'd barricaded on the side closest to the outer wall with sacks of flour and grain. Others had taken shelter in his kitchen behind him, and Rachel was clinging to her dolly beneath the counter by his side.

No one had expected such a massacre, not now, not the week after a holiday. And for a bread dealer, Diarmuid was dangerously low to running out of food for the inhabitants of his little shop turned fortress. They comprised trapped customers, the postman and the occasional wounded passer-by they'd pulled from the danger of the street, two of which had already died in the back room.

But, for now, there was relative peace. Shaking, Diarmuid whispered to Rachel to stay put and rose to rocking feet. The survivors clutched their rosaries, saying their hushed prayers while they could. The young Miss McNicholas, a local school teacher, was dusting down her dress and rearranging her hair with the help of the cracked window. And, but for that window, his shop, his home, was still intact.

He was just about to sigh with relief at his good fortune when she gasped and jumped back from the window.

'Soldier!'

Diarmuid braced himself against the counter and swallowed. His eyes flickered to a stale baguette beside him on the counter; not the best weapon, but there nonetheless. Not a moment later, the bell chimed and the door creaked open.

His heart all but stopped as the soldier stepped inside and took off his hat.

'Morning, Diarmuid!'

He swallowed, his throat dry. 'Dónal. The usual?'

Dónal swept his hair down, freeing his dark curls of ash. Diarmuid tried not to look at the trail of dried blood that ran from his forehead and down the side of his dusty face. 'Not today. Connolly sent me for bread. Got a white loaf, by chance? We're starved!'

'Not the only ones,' Tommy Brennan grumbled from his place under the display table. Dónal's head snapped around.

'Postman!' His attention panned throughout the room as Diarmuid rolled one of his last white loaves into some paper. 'Ah, Miss!'

'You should be at school,' Miss McNicholas said, her voice firm. 'You have a history essay on the American colonies to complete by Friday.'

Dónal shrugged. 'Why learn history when you can write it, Miss?'

That riled the others. Diarmuid hurried the rest of his wrapping and handed the loaf over. Dónal set his hat back on his head and fumbled about in his pocket for the necessary coins. Ignoring the deathly silence that had befallen the shop, Diarmuid fetched a jar from the shelves behind the counter and prised it open.

As Dónal handed over the money, Diarmuid caught his hand and slipped a penny toffee into his palm in its place.

'Stay safe,' he whispered, holding his gaze. Dónal closed his fingers around it and smiled, softly this time. He pulled back and tipped his hat at Rachel, who still had to stand on the very tips of her toes to see him over the counter.

Diarmuid watched him go with a lump in his throat. He stroked Rachel's hair, the same mousy brown as her mother's - God rest her soul – as Dónal shut the door behind him, making the little bell sing.

They both knew he wouldn't be back for another toffee penny.

He sighed and reached for the day's newspaper again. What else could they do?

'Get down!'

The voice on the quay was muffled, but Diarmuid heard it all the same. With barely a thought to it, he pushed Rachel back beneath the counter and followed, clutching her tight.

A thundering shot resounded throughout the quay. The window shattered, spraying the room in shards of glass. Diarmuid crushed Rachel against himself, putting her between his body and the floor as she screamed. Another shot went off, this time landing somewhere else along the street. It took Diarmuid a moment to realise that they weren't single shots, but rounds upon rounds of shells, sailing into the streets and raising screams from the passers-by.

The shelves behind them splintered and partly collapsed, sending most of Diarmuid's neatly arranged bottles crashing to the floor. Something sharp pricked at his heel; he clutched Rachel closer.

Something must have hit his home above the shop, because as the shots moved away and cheers replaced them, the ceiling creaked. Diarmuid pushed himself upright, bringing Rachel with him. For a long moment, they sat together, hardly daring to breathe as they listened to the crying and cracks of guns.

'Stay here,' he murmured, pressing a kiss into her hair and her dolly into her hands. She wasn't crying, but she nodded and snuffled into the doll's cotton dress.

He straightened upright to check on the others in the back room, picking his way through the shards of glass and wooden splinters; this was at very least salvageable. The three he'd taken in were cocooned under a makeshift bomb shelter of shelves and chairs.

'Is everyone all right in here?' he hissed, as though anything louder would bring it all back, would make his home and business the main target instead of the GPO and Liberty Hall. He was met with a series of nods.

'That must have been the gunboat,' Jimmy Piper from next door muttered. 'I heard some rumours from a couple of pigs yesterday. They called it the Helga.'

'Whatever it was, I'm sure it's gone now. Seems like it's sailed on.' He cast his eyes upwards as the ceiling creaked again. 'I'm almost afraid to see what's been done up there.'

'We should get out,' said a second, a woman Jimmy had hauled in and bandaged the arm of just yesterday. Diarmuid was no longer fond of learning their names; it only made it more painful when they died. 'If it went up, surely it has to come back down!'

Diarmuid's feet locked to the spot of their own accord. 'The door is through there if you wish to do so, but I won't be following you. Three generations this shop has been in my family; it won't end with me. Besides, it's a front line out there. We're much safer inside.'

Another creak from above.

'Are you sure about that?'

'Of course! Now, who's hungry? I have—'

Some higher power must have been conspiring against him, because the next thing he knew, his voice was joining the screams in the street as the ceiling crashed to the ground. Diarmuid berated himself later for being unable to remember anything but the crushing darkness and the smell of stone and dust that flooded his senses. Pressed against the floor beneath the weight of his own ceiling, his eyes watered against the particles and he shuttered them.

He wasn't sure how long it was until he opened them, but it was to the sounds of voices, voices he didn't fully recognise. Something was dragged off his back, giving him room to breathe, and light flooded his little cave. Then there were arms and hands, and he was being hauled from the rubble by three men, their voices loud and blurry to listen to.

Diarmuid draped his arms across two pairs of shoulders and let them take his weight. They led him through a new hole in the wall, the door to the shop front blocked by the fallen ceiling. His ears rang, loud whistles that shut out the reassurances his saviours were giving and his head spun as he hit the fresh air. He blinked away the dust in his eyes.

They set him at the side of the river, his legs dangling off the quay. When he looked closer, he noticed the thin layer of dust had settled on the surface of the water.

'Where's Rachel?' he managed to wheeze as one of the men handed him a cloth, dampened with the tea from his flask. Diarmuid cleaned his face, only half shocked to see it come away streaked with crimson like a grisly watercolour.

'Still looking,' the other said. 'But they did find this on the road.'

Diarmuid tried not to flinch as he was handed Rachel's dolly. A sharp nod was all he could manage before he cleared his throat.

'Find her.'

'We'll try.'

It took three days to clear the shop, three days in which he listened to the sounds of gunfire and the wailing that pierced the air every so often. He took refuge further inland at night, only returning to the quay to see if they'd recovered his little girl.

He was rewarded with her body on the Saturday.

The rebels didn't notice him as they marched to their surrender. Diarmuid caught Pearse's eye for just a moment as he and Elizabeth O'Farrell walked with their heads high to arrange talks with the British. They didn't stop as they passed the grieving father holding his little girl's body on the other side of the road. Diarmuid was almost tempted to spit as they passed by, but his strength failed him, and he returned to his grieving. Instead, he gently tied the necklace around Rachel's neck, kissing her forehead and whispering useless nothings.

He learned later that around 450 people had died throughout the week, including young Dónal Flanagan when the GPO had gone up in flames. More were wounded and Dublin had been reduced to a shell of its former self.

Diarmuid buried Rachel with her dolly in the following week. He settled for nothing less than resting her next to her mother and spent his days sitting with them in the silence that the rising had draped over the city. Those who he met didn't recognise him, for the events of the week had aged him almost ten years, and the few that did kept quiet.

Then came the executions. Diarmuid didn't care for most; after all, these men had taken his one hope in life, and what did he care for theirs? But then came the news of the dying Connolly and the young Plunkett. Then the threat of the fierce Markievicz's death hit his ears, and all tolerance Diarmuid O'Rourke had for Westminster's hold over his people ebbed away.

His Ireland would never be the same again.

Overcoming the Border

By Liam Woodgate, age 16.

Borders
They can lock us in
Or keep us out
All the while we lay down
And let their walls grow
higher and higher
brick by brick
The borders of the mind

I sit and watch as you shatter and crumble
Until all your dust is gone with the wind

I sit and watch
Doing nothing more than hoping
That you may rebuild yourself
That you may be helped

I sit and watch
As you never truly know how much you are worth
How your dust is made of solid gold

How you are loved.

But let your mind be shattered

Let the walls be built
Around the happy child you are

And let the barbed wire
Coil around and around
Higher and higher
Until the end is a noose
that you tied yourself

You surrender to yourself
Without a truce
Unholy trinity of me
Myself and I
In contempt of the happy child you are
That no one knows
Until the day that you die.

Or

Take my hand
Break free
Come with me
And know what it's like to be
Happy

I stand and scream with you
To break the resolve of your borders
When nobody else will do anything but watch

I stand and stay with you

As every trip, every fall and every time you fail

Gets pushed back in the face of your border

I stand and fight with you

When you are at your weakest

But you aren't weak

You are you!

I stand and hold your hand

As the borders and fences fall in the face of all these trials you overcame

I stand and watch with you

The world we made together.

Praise Song for Gaga

By Ciara Dowling, age 17.

You are
the canary's song to me
sweet, subdued, melodious

You are
the moon to me
gravitating, guiding, resilient,

You are
a flamingo to me
flashing, flamboyant, unreserved

You are
the orange tree to me
a summer pool to me
air conditioning to me

'They can't scare me, if I scare them first,' you said.

Inspired by 'Praise Song For My Mother' by Grace Nichols

Pieces of Time

By Aoife Lennon, age 17.

The steady beep of a machine. The soft weeping of family members who know what's coming. The halting huff of breath from the frail figure on the bed, who is slowly slipping into sleep...

...

The dark wood floor was cool beneath him. He wriggled around, two-year-old limbs clumsy and uncoordinated. He managed to stand, toddling uncertainly toward the soft backlit figure of his mother. Hearing his little steps, she turned around and, beaming, crouched and held out her arms. The baby giggled and lurched forward, losing his balance. The ground rushed up to meet him, but his mother's arms were there and he landed right in them, still laughing. The front door closed and in walked his father with a smile on his face. The small boy lit up, 'Dada!', and wobbled toward the man. His father scooped him up and lifted him over his head. In a whirl of light and colour, the scene changes.

He was still young, maybe three then, and he was tucked in his little cot. The room was dark, lit only by moonlight from a nearby window. Angry voices floated through the air, coming from his parents' room across the hall. He heard loud approaching footsteps and smelled whiskey. He'd been smelling that a lot recently. He huddled under his blanket shivering as the footsteps intensified, and then passed. A door slammed and he heard crying from the other room. Maybe a minute, maybe an hour later, he heard quiet footsteps and he shut his eyes, knowing in his heart that he shouldn't be awake. Someone came to the crib, and simply stood there for the longest time. Then, cool fingers brushed his hair from his face and his mother whispered, 'What are we going to do?'...

...

The elderly man in the bed awakens with a hacking cough, still thinking of his parents. His children crowd around him offering concern and calling for a nurse. His energy is fading again already as he drifts back into sleep.

...

The headmaster of the local boys' school was an imposing man even when he was in a good mood. When he was in a bad mood, you knew to keep your head down or else risk the dreaded cane. The young boy, who was about eight, knew this as he had learned it the hard way. However, for all the times he had faced the master's wrath, he had never seen him look quite as dangerous as he did today. The boy slid down in his seat until his chin touched his chest, not daring to look up at the great fire-breathing dragon before him.

'Do you know, boy,' the headmaster said, imperiously, 'why you are here?'

The headmaster did everything imperiously, and had great fondness for rhetorical questions. The boy didn't know this, and opened his mouth to answer but was cut off sharply by the master, 'Speak only when spoken to, boy!' Another thing about the headmaster was that he liked to call all the students (and some of the teachers as well), 'boy'. The young boy hung his head.

'The answer, boy,' snapped the master, 'is that you have been fighting! Besmirching our schoolyard like a common thug!'

The boy knew what he is referring to. The day before, some boys on the playground had made some derogatory comments about his mother, and he had been forced to shut them up with force. He had managed to blame his dusty clothes and split lip on a fall from the pavement when he had gone home that evening, but the master wasn't so easily fooled.

'Well, boy?' thundered the master, spraying the young boy with spittle. 'What have you to say for yourself?'

The boy mumbled something.

'Speak up!'

'They called me Ma a whore.'

The master drew himself up to his full height, flushing red. You could almost see the sparks flying from him. Hope ignited inside the young boy

111

– surely the other boys would now be punished and they wouldn't dare insult his mother again!

'And now you add foul language to your list of crimes! How dare you use that word in my presence? Give me your hand! It's the cane for you, boy!'

The boy's mother frowned as she listened to his story and bandaged his hand.

'I know,' she said, 'that you meant well. But please, try to keep your head down and ignore hooligans like that. Don't go getting on the master's bad side more than you can help.'

The young boy didn't understand, but he resolved to listen to his mother's words.

...

The elderly man's eyes fluttered open. The room around him had taken on a too-bright, ethereal quality. He could have sworn that the walls had used to be green. They now seemed a pale blue. No matter, he decided, he was too tired to think about such trivial things...

...

He was fresh out of college when the war came. He was young and carefree, surrounded by friends and he hardly ever wanted for anything. The summer days were long and warm and he was invincible. When tidings of a dictator came from overseas, it seemed like a great opportunity. The horrors of the first Great War had faded into old stories told in the same tone as those about ghosts and Bigfoot and so the young man and his comrades eagerly signed up for the army, relishing the glory that was sure to come. They wore their crisp uniforms with pride, the ladies flocked around them, the autumn days were long and cool and it seemed that the war was a long way off. Then the dictator stepped up his campaign. The high life of a man in uniform dissolved overnight, leaving the young man in a fight for his life and his country almost every day. He grew thin and gaunt from stress and lack of sleep. His eyes grew haunted with the souls of the fellow soldiers that he saw blasted out of the sky every day, and in his ears, the anguished cries of the loved ones left behind, the sobs of children who had lost their homes and the screams of his best friends as they perish in the blaze of a bomb dropped by a Nazi plane, rang out like that accursed air raid siren, night and day. The winter nights were long and painful and seemed like they would never end. Only when the sun peeked over the horizon, did the enemy bombers disappear back to where they came from. Often, they would come back during the day as well. This seemed to go on forever and the young man began to question why he decided to put himself through this in the first place, and if it would ever end. Even death, he concluded, would be better than enduring this for one more minute. The end of the war eventually arrived with the suicide of the dictator and although all those around him danced and kissed and rejoiced the end of the torment, the young man couldn't even bring himself to smile. The spring days were long and colourless without those who used to give them their vibrancy...

...

The old man awakens again, his heart full of memories and his eyes full of tears. The room is still hazy, its occupants indistinct. This time, he isn't even awake long enough to form a coherent thought before he falls back into the twilight of his dreams...

...

After the war, he floated through life as though he were a ghost, as dead as those he had lost. This grey half-life was only made worse by the sudden death of his mother. The doctors assured him that it had been painless in the end, '...a heart attack, unfortunate and rare for a woman so young, absolutely painless, she didn't suffer at all...'

A hollow comfort to the man. He had returned to his mother's apartment, his childhood home, but the ghosts of his past still roamed the corridors at night so he spent more and more of his time outdoors until eventually he refused to return to the flat at all, preferring to spend his nights in the open air, where the dreams of the stiflingly warm plane cockpit couldn't wake him, gasping, at all hours of the night. He could feel himself spiralling downhill, jumping at loud, sharp noises, unable to go near the harbour over which so many battles had taken place and eventually escaping to the bottom of a bottle where the faces of his loved ones couldn't find him. It was in this state, hysterical and scraping rock bottom, that he met Gladys. Passed out in the gutter, barely breathing, someone had called an ambulance for him. When he woke up, he thought he had died. Standing over him, was a stunning creature, dressed in white, with a halo of golden hair. When he asked her if she was an angel, she raised her eyebrows and replied that, no, she wasn't an angel, but she got that a lot, and for goodness sake, couldn't you have chosen a more original pickup line. At this he smiled for the first time in months, and told her he would try harder next time she picked him out the gutter. Her only response was a quick half-smile, that lit her whole face and he knew that he wanted to keep seeing that smile for the rest of his life. She nursed him through the next few weeks and slowly, she began to smile at him more and more. When she found out there was no-one in the outside world to visit him, she began to spend her lunch breaks at his bedside. He cherished those hours spent with her, and when the time came for him to leave the hospital and go back to his flat, he was surprised to find that he didn't want to leave. In a fit of awkward desperation, he asked her if, maybe, only if she wanted to of course, perhaps, did she want to go out for dinner with him sometime? She watched him shrewdly throughout this halting proposal and for a second he thought he had made a horrible mistake, but then she smiled that wonderful smile and said she'd think about it. A week later and they'd had their first date. A month later, they'd made it official, and a year later, they were married. Three children followed and the flat, which was now a much warmer and sunnier place to the man, (who was by now rapidly approaching middle-age) simply wasn't big enough anymore. They moved into a small house on the outskirts of town and lived happily there ever since...

...

The old man awakens, smiling. Ah, Gladys. How he misses her. She had died two years previously. A single tear slides down the old man's cheek as he thinks about how he will see her soon. Very soon... he lets out his last breath. The monitor beside him emits one long continuous beep. He is gone.

...

The man opens his eyes to a beautiful, blonde-haired woman standing over him. He reaches up and takes her hand. Close by, a stately middle-aged woman is talking to a group of mischievous-looking young men in military dress uniforms. Upon seeing him, they all rise to greet him with grins and embraces. The man smiles. He is home at last.

On Leaving

By Richard Enright, age 17.

The word 'brave' comes to mind, and then leaves;

It leaves like most things have and will

If time is really an illusion, why can I feel its hand on my ankle now?
Pulling me onwards, eastwards,

Forcing the word 'goodbye' from my mouth.
the others come so easy, you know that well,

It hurts
For now.

It will leave like most things have and will;
There's nothing I can do.

The pain will pass from me, only the poems will remain

To hurt me then
As this parting hurts me now.

The Ship

By Joshua Gordon O'Gorman, age 17.

The red light blinked at me. Recording. I must get the message out.
Something was wrong. Maybe someone, somewhere would receive my
signal, but I couldn't be certain.

'The events I am about to outline may shock you,' I begin, 'if you even
hear this at all. It is my only hope. My name is Jeremy Grace, and I am
floating endlessly through space…'

It all began in the academy.

As a young boy, I had been fascinated with space. Every year, I visited
various aeronautic galleries, exhibits, displays, and seminars, from the age
of five. The stars were my friends, comforting me when no one else
would. My parents liked to leave me with the stars; they were unable to
really understand me. They could see me look up at night, and stare at the
round white face of the moon, and ponder the vastness of the universe. I
was still a child, but I had a great imagination. There was something out
there, I knew it. And I wanted to find it, whatever it was.

I was non-verbal until the age of thirteen. I either couldn't speak, or chose
not to, or so I was told. I was able to talk sometimes, but never to people.
I could talk to the stars. They would listen and never judge me, even with
my strangest, most abstract thoughts. We shared secrets, the stars and
myself. Sometimes I could even hear them talk to me.

But even my parents never heard me speak. I would sometimes write or
draw what I wanted or needed, or usually I would point and hum. My
parents did their best. My mum was always kind, and patient, but she
didn't always know what to do. Many nights I woke up, from some dream
or another, and descend the stairs, in search of her comfort, and I found
her crying, desperate to be able to 'fix' me. As if I needed fixing. It always
hurt me, a little, to hear her like that.

My father was different. He was helpful, but he was not as patient as my mother. He would never hurt me, but he would lose his temper and shout when he couldn't understand me. I preferred how he dealt with me. I was able to deal with his yelling, but my mother's sobs cut me deep.

But the stars were the best. They gave me support, and they were my safety. I relied on them for my own personal peace. It was outdoors, beneath a sky that sparkled, filled with millions of glittering diamonds, that I found my tongue. My only companion at that time was my only friend, a boy named Rick. He had come to my house, and he sat out with me. I feel he pitied me more than befriended me, but nonetheless he was there, and even if it were only pity, I still trusted him.

'Look at them,' I said to him, and pointed upwards. Rick almost jumped at hearing my voice. He turned to me and his eyes opened wider than a barn door

'Jeremy!' he exclaimed. 'You just spoke!'

I looked back at him, and it was only then I realised I had said anything at all. 'Yes,' I said warily. 'I know how, I just never do.'

'Oh my god!' he said, and it was my turn to jump. He had almost shouted in my ear, and it shocked me back into my perpetual silence.

From that moment on, I could speak to Rick as well as the stars. I told him the things that annoyed me, the way I'd seen friends do in movies. We hung out, and I shared my love of the sky with him. He became as interested as I was, and often we would sit and examine the night, searching for abnormalities and constellations, naming new ones ourselves.

It was the summer of my eighteenth birthday that we enrolled in the academy together. Each of us had received some of the highest results in a nationwide exam, and so we were invited to become explorers in space, by the New World Space Organisation, or NWSO. When I opened the letter, I almost exploded with elation. I had passed the physical tests (barely) and I was the second highest result on the panel. They told us that we, as the first cosmonauts of the New Order, would go further into space than any other humans had ever been.

The New Order was always beneficial, in some ways, or so we had always learned. When the Third Great War had destroyed many countries, and the world's population was almost halved, the New Order had risen from the ashes of a tired world to take control. They were benevolent, and they expanded until they covered all of Europe, North America, some of Southern and Eastern Asia, and the Arctic. The only issue with the New Order was that the leaders were corrupt. Every last one of them.

If certain countries wanted special illegal permissions, the New Order would never reject a bribe. If there was a disaster, it was common for it to mysteriously disappear out of record, while an economic boom seemed to occur all throughout, fed by surreptitious payments made through non-existent accounts. The New Order were clever, and they were rich. None of that mattered to me, however, as I would soon be leaving to explore the universe.

We trained hard at the academy. The various NWSO specialists each gave us courses in their fields. We were put into five teams of six, the number used on each space journey. I was in a group with Rick. I specialised in spacecraft mechanical operations, meaning I flew the spaceship, and performed any special repairs. There was the nutrition specialist, Jean, the physical expert, Anthony, the deputy mechanic, Laura (who worked wherever I was unable, and doing more minor repairs), the analyst, Simon, and of course our ground control correspondent. Rick worked in ground control. He had to communicate with the team about any information he was receiving, any errors, and any anomalies in the analysts' findings.

In the time I was training I had learned to be more open, though I was still rather reserved. At least I was able to communicate with my team, and that was the important part of our work.

I was unable to believe my luck. The NWSO were allowing me to go to the place I had spent my life dreaming of, imagining, talking to and relying on. My mind was filled with wonderful fantasies of the universe, and the mysteries it might hold.

A few days before I was to depart this world, I received two visits. The first was decidedly more unexpected than the second; my parents. They had travelled from the north of Scotland all the way to the Tokyo Space Centre. At least that's what it would have been called before the New Order; they no longer distinguished country borders, though they understood the cultural significance of recognising various nationalities within its reaches. I was shocked they had come.

'Jeremy,' my mother said to me, 'I'm so glad you get to live your dream! Space travel! My little boy is an astronaut!'

My father looked at me, silent, but I could see the hint of pride in his eyes. He opened his mouth to speak, but seemed not to know what words to use.

My mother extended her arms to hug me, and I recoiled for a moment. She withheld, understanding that I needed to agree to let her touch me. I hesitated, then reached forward for an uncomfortable few seconds. She embraced me tightly, and I didn't move. She then released me, and I could see the tears streaming from her eyes.

'We're going to miss you,' she said, and she put her hand into her pocket, producing a handkerchief. She blew her nose noisily, and then replaced the handkerchief in her coat. Her eyes were red and puffy now. My dad's face was more solemn, and he looked at me with a sadness that I had never seen before. In that moment I saw a new side to my father, one that cared about me and my achievements, not my weakness and dependency. I felt a surge of emotion, waves crashing over me, and I broke down crying, for the very first time in my life.

My parents stayed for an hour or more. I couldn't tell exactly, as my sense of time was disturbed by their appearance and the lack of a clock in the visitation centre. They realised, as well as I did, that this was likely the last time they'd see me for a long time, if ever. Every moment of that day was special to them, and to me, though I didn't understand how much so yet. It would take some time for me to fully be able to comprehend the gravity of the visit.

When my parents left, I was visited by another man. He wore a grey suit, had grey hair, and in the light, seemingly a grey face, all of which represented his personality with perfect accuracy. Accompanying him was an odour of what I can only describe as cigarette smoke mixed with whiskey, two smells I had become somewhat accustomed to at the academy, though still found unbearable and suffocating.

'Hello, Jeremy,' he said. He extended his hand, but I didn't take it. 'I'm Reginald Freeman, head of the New Order Resource Committee.' His hand hung in the air, like a bad odour, and still I did not reach for it. He lowered it again, and cleared his throat. 'Not well versed in the pleasantries, I see. Well then, I might as well get straight down to business.'

He sat down tentatively in one of the chairs, as if it might contaminate him. He gestured for me to sit. I was still shook from my parents visit. I had been expecting someone of this sort to arrive into my room. I remained standing.

He ignored my rejection of his offer, and opened the briefcase he held in his left hand. He pulled from it a paper, and on the top I could see printed the words 'Resource Committee Expansion and Harvesting.' He examined it for a moment, and then looked back at me, and seemed to only notice then that I was still standing.

'Jeremy, you are one of the brightest minds in the entire New Order. I'm delighted to be able to say that you get to be one of the first humans to explore outside the solar system. I, as head of the Resource Committee, have been asked to pass you this document. I've been told to give you some time to review it, and return to me with an answer in, let's say, two hours.' He handed me the sheet.

I took it, though reluctantly. I flipped it and read the first few lines. 'You want me to steal resources,' I said aloud.

'Oh no, don't think of it like that!' he interrupted, acting flustered, though the words sounded practised. 'Think of it as reallocation of goods.' He looked at me expectantly.

'It's stealing,' I said to him flatly. For once, I was glad that my mind worked how it did; everything had an order, a definition, a right and a wrong. Stealing was wrong. Killing was wrong. Smiling was right. It was simple. For me it was black and white. For Reginald, it was grey, just as his attire.

'Well, it seems you don't find this mutually beneficial' he said, realising he wasn't going to get anywhere. 'Shall I give you the time to mull it over? Or have you already made up your mind?'

'I don't steal!' I said to him. Why did I have to talk so much? I was exhausted. I looked at him, and motioned at the door.

'Very well' he said, and with a sweeping motion, he stood up, spun around and almost stormed out of the room, containing his contempt with his held breath and a sharp posture. His grey coat tail fluttered behind him.

The rest of the day passed uneventfully.

The morning of the launch, I was up two hours before dawn, unable to sleep with my nervous stomach. 'I should have slept more' I mumbled to myself. I was sitting outside the Training Centre, looking up at the night sky.

'Look at them,' said a voice to my left. I turned and saw Rick standing, pointing at the stars. He smiled at me, and sat down beside me. 'I knew you'd be here' he said as he settled himself into a comfortable position. 'You don't have to talk' he assured me. 'I hear you got a visit yesterday.'

My mind flicked to Reginald Freeman, and a sense of unease rose within me. I shifted around, trying to settle myself. The thought of that man made me feel like a child standing in front of a hall full of people and having to give a speech – tremendously uncomfortable.

'Your mum and dad came all the way from Edinburgh.' For some reason I cannot explain, I felt a sense of relief when he didn't mention the Head of the Resource Committee. 'It must have been some shock,' he continued. 'It probably took almost a day to get here.'

I nodded, not moving my gaze from the sky. I felt at ease in that moment. The sky, the stars and my best friend brought me a great sense of joy and relaxation. Rick stopped speaking, and just let me sit there beside him, taking in the scene. I pointed at certain stars, and he would follow the trail of my finger and try to see the brightest ones in the sky.

We were called to our stations after an hour, or thereabouts, of this. The excitement rose in my stomach again, and I found myself almost skipping to the changing rooms. The five of us got changed into our outfits, ready for our adventure; Rick would be staying on Earth, monitoring our progress. No one spoke as we got dressed. We each had our own silent thoughts and worries. We were supposed to be a tight unit, and have a special bond, for security and our own sanity, but some things are best left unspoken.

I progressed onto the ship, with the rest of the crew. We settled into our seats, and awaited the inevitable thrill of the countdown. 10, 9, 8… No training could prepare me for the sense of dread that flooded me as I heard the voice counting backwards. So many things could go wrong. 7, 6, 5… But I was also excited. It was my lifelong dream! I would be near the stars. 4, 3, 2, 1… It was time.

…

Three months in space can change your perception of reality. There is no night. There is no weight. Nothing is normal.

I could always see the stars. I took great comfort in the fact that they were perpetually present in my waking moments. I could look out the window of our ship and feel the same way I felt every time I saw them – happy. It was an odd sensation.

The food was terrible but I was expecting that. All food in space is powdered versions of real food, and much more tasteless. I missed the flavour of a good lasagne, or my mother's roast potatoes. Even some bad chips would have been welcome. Instead I got powdered milk, the dusty essence of vegetables and a breath of what may once have been meat. It was my only real complaint, however.

Then one day, things went downhill at a rapid pace.

I was pacing in my quarters, filling my time between reading the books I had. I had turned on the gravity field, allowing the crew to walk and exercise as they would on earth. At some point, I can't recall exactly when, I went for a wander about the ship. I had still only explored a small amount of it, given its enormous size. It was as long as six or seven football fields all laid end to end, by another six across in width; it was simply massive.

Pacing the white reflective corridors, I was suddenly struck by a familiar smell I couldn't quite place. It was a strong odour, unbearable. Something I had smelt not too long ago, some foul scent. Like cigarettes and whiskey, I thought to myself. It was coming from a room that I had never seen – a common occurrence. I slid my hand to the panel that would open the door, and a red light flashed on the screen. I was startled for a second. Red? The lights were always green.

'Restricted access' flashed on the screen in red capital letters. I was perplexed. I had never had restricted access in any part of the academy or ship before. Why this room? The smell was much stronger now and it almost burned my nostrils. Where had I smelt it before?

I tried the door again. The same message jumped out at me. I heard movement on the other side of the sealed door, and I stepped back. I ducked around the corner just as the familiar hiss of the hydraulic seal told me the door had opened.

There was the sound of a few footsteps, echoing down the empty halls. I saw a grey shadow cast in fluorescent light on the wall. I was going to confront whoever had been in the room, but instinct told me against it, and as always, I listened to it. The shadow turned away from me and went walking the other way along with its owner. I waited until the clack of shoes had faded away entirely, and walked around the corner. There were no signs of the other person. Who had it been? Did we have a stowaway?

The door was still open. Things were getting stranger and stranger. I opened it, and peered inside. There was almost nothing there. Almost.

In the centre of the room was a machine of some sort, which will require a great deal of description. Made of the same material as the interior of our ship, it was reflective and white. It had three distinct sides, each one situated around a central cylinder, with a triangular curve between each side. On the face that pointed at me was mounted a screen. There was something displayed on it I couldn't quite work out. It looked vaguely humanoid, but it was missing limbs. There were several diagrams, and snatches of writing, in an almost illegible script around it. There was one very clear phrase. 'Genetic mutations – superhumans'.

'What?' I muttered aloud. I very quickly memorised all that I could. An odour drifted into the room. The same smell of cigarettes and whiskey I had smelt earlier. I spun around.

'Hello, Jeremy,' said Reginald Freeman. 'I suspected I'd find you in here, snooping around. You seem like a clever bloke, but just not quite clever enough.'

'What do you mean?' I said, refusing to let my voice betray my mind. I was startled, and furious. How had I not remembered the hideous smell immediately? I should have realised it was this ratty little man much earlier.

'What I mean is unimportant now, Jeremy. You should be much more frightened. The New Order doesn't employ just anyone here.'

'Why are you here?' I interjected.

'Because I can be, and because I want to be.'

I was struck by the simplicity and bluntness of his answer. What on earth was happening? How had he gotten onto my ship? I realised then that there must have been a traitor among either the crew or ground control. No one else had access to the lower holds, and we had been in the cockpit at launch.

'What, are you lost for words?' he asked me.

I didn't answer. I found myself once more trapped inside myself. I longed so badly for the comfort of the stars, to let me get this all out, and to let them speak back.

'The stars?' he said to me. 'Oh, poor boy. The stars won't save you this time. You're still a child. And yes, I can read your mind,' he added, as an afterthought.

I managed a feeble 'how?'

'That's none of your business,' he said to me. 'Now, it's time you left.'

From his pocket he produced what looked like a small pen. He lunged forward and jabbed it into my leg. The world blurred into one mass of colour, and the last thing I saw was Reginald Freeman's smile twist and distort until his face no longer looked human at all. In fact, it was almost like the drawing on the screen.

I woke up in my quarters, and only small glimpses of the memory swam around in my head. I looked about my room for any reminders, anything to help me recover the missing parts. I remembered the drawing and the screen, but where were they? Who had been there? Details jumped about and looked to fill themselves in.

I stood and checked my messages. Rick had told me that one of the pods was having issues, and that I had to go check it. What issues could they have been? I was uncertain but I went anyway. I called him and he told me there was a power issue; he claimed one of the supply lines from the generator was faulty and that the pod was sending inconsistent error reports.

I headed to the pods, and I made a quick check outside. The generator was reading to be ok, as was the power line for each pod. I entered one of them, and made a few routine checks. I still couldn't find an error, so I checked each one in turn. In the final one, I was almost finished my check when the power cut. The generator didn't kick in either. Despair rose inside me. I knew something was wrong.

It struck me. The horrendous odour clung to my nose for a second, as if it was imaginary. Reginald Freeman. He had been on the ship. He was researching some form of genetic mutation. For years I had heard rumours of the government performing tests on young orphaned children, to see how the effects of various chemicals and levels of radiations affected them in later life. Those that survived the tests were often disabled. Few had been mentally stable enough to tell of their time in the facilities, and each of those was later discredited by a 'private body.' I had never believed them to be true. I thought that the people who tried to tell us were just looking for attention or money.

Now, I was certain it was true, and I knew that I was going to be destroyed for it. He had decided to let me live last night, but realised he had to kill me.

The power turned on again. The pod door was sealed. I tried to open it, to no avail. I checked the information screen. There was a small-scale representation of the pods, each represented by a green glow. As I watched, each pod was launched in turn. Five lights. Four. Three. When the second light went out, I knew I was done for.

I felt the release of the pod from the ship. I looked out the window, and I could see the ship, floating behind me like a feather as it falls to earth, moving gently and slowly. The stars were racing past me. The stars. How I wished for them to rescue me. How I longed for their comfort. How I wanted them to tell me why I was being punished.

...

'... and that is my entire story. I hope this reaches someone. Maybe I'll be rescued. I have enough provisions to last maybe another few months, if I'm careful. Wish me luck. And if anyone on Earth does happen to come across this broadcast, please find Rick Whitespoon. He'll know what to do.'

The video cut out. A hand gently closed the laptop screen. Rick had watched the video twice now. He started to laugh, just a little.

'Foolish Jeremy,' he said to the empty room. 'You were always gonna get yourself into something like this.'

He opened the laptop again, and he moved the cursor. It hovered over the icon of a bin for a moment. 'Are you sure you want to delete this file? Once deleted, it cannot be recovered.' The screen prompted him. 'Yes.'

The only copy of Jeremy's broadcast was gone. Rick laughed for a minute. 'The stars,' he chuckled to himself. 'He really was a nuisance. He's gone at last.' Rick relaxed a moment, and the room filled with the odour of cigarettes and whiskey as Reginald Freeman's face appeared where Rick's had been only seconds before. 'The fool.'

In the Mourning

By Orla Browne, age 17.

She kept trying to give us all painkillers,
which I didn't understand
because
we were going to hurt
a lot, regardless, and to be
numb would have been worse
than the guarantee of tears.
At least that's what I thought,
but I watched them be
graciously accepted by shaking hands
and swallowed like pills of
salvation.
It was supposed to be sad,
I insisted, and I couldn't bear
the thought of not
being sad at all. So
I said no,
politely,
and turned them down. Deciding
there was enough death
already without killing pain
as well.

I am a Poet

By Emma Ryan, age 16.

I am a poet.

A craftsman of comprehension,

A welder of words.

I've created my own remix

Shaping words into sentences,

Sentences into poems

The same words that make you laugh,

I twist to make you cry.

I make you see the world through my eyes

You cannot see the image stored in my head

But I'll do my best to describe every knot in the tree

Every spice in the air

Each footfall

As though you were right there beside me.

Through poetry I can tell you my thoughts,

By drastic change of pace you can tell

My heart quickens my pulse races and my heart pumps.

But then,

I slow,

And you follow

Just like a dance.

With you following,

I lead you in beauty and in grace,

Still a timed beat to be kept

The words my tempo.

By my concentration alone you can guess,

From the mottled grey leaves of autumn and bowing branches of

squirrel!

My imagination is unlocked and you see what I do,

That rusty coated creature clutching acorns to its chest

With a beard.

Blonde streaks its body from his chin to his toes,

I laugh.

And as I have not said this aloud

People look at me with deep confusion

Possibly sympathy

For I have just looked at a tree and laughed.

They did not live in my moment

They missed Dumbledore balancing on a branch.

I am a poet

And I write so I can share these rare moments with you.

Because if I don't

I'm just laughing at a tree.

The Four-Beat Sin

By Tola Ní Shúilleabháin, age 16.

Dear Reader, my name is Gustave Neumann and, for reasons prescribed by the madman our desperate country has begun to lionize, I am not a good German boy. I want more than anything to be a composer and yet I know that this will never happen. Dear reader, let me show you my music.

I sit on the big rock and wait for him.

The din of the river Lucca had once brought me to, rushing intently, provides a steady bass to the forest song. Above it the clarion chirping of birds emanate from everywhere like an omnipresent choir. My presence does not affect the vocalists; they are at ease in my company.

I hear Lucca before I see him; the crackle of dry leaves, twigs and nettle in 1/ 2 timing. I remember his face as he approaches and his hands stuffed awkwardly into his trouser pockets. Suddenly those hands are touching my face, my jaw and my neck. It's an abrupt, uncomfortable hello and then I begin to kiss Lucca back.

Coming up for air I smile and greet him, taking his hand in mine, squeezing gently and running my thumb up and down over his knuckles. I remember his veins like thin pale blue branches showing faintly beneath the skin. The hand was warm and a little moist with sweat; he was always nervous at first. I think a small part of Lucca still looked on at him and me, at us and our delicate situation, with horror and disgust refusing to believe that it had anything to do with the feelings and deeds of its host body. That small part just wants to be normal and much as I hate it in Lucca I could not help but feel pity for the boy that I loved. Lucca Volkmar the Good German boy.

Listen closely, Reader, for the music is at its most faint and poignant. So sudden and yet so vivid- the four beat bar before an explosive chorus. There was something eerie about the silence between Lucca and me that day and I remember kissing his lips softly, barely even touching the skin, in an almost brotherly act of affection to ease his tremoring hands and the strange guilt that I could see flying behind his eyes. I just wanted to make it okay- to tell him that whatever else may be, here and now was okay. I was going to say something, to put what I felt and meant into words when the first beat in that abominable bar came. Not so far away something large in the bushes curses with the pain of a nettle sting. The next beat came as I looked up sharply into Lucca's big brown eyes and our gazes locked in mutual terror. His hand broke away from mine as Lucca jumped up. Finally that last minor note twanged as we saw the shadowy figure of man darting through the trees.

This melody is my curse. Its sinful beauty, its perfect crime will play through my conscience eternally.

Dear reader, I am engulfed.

Ode to my Crockery

By Sadhbh Goodwin, age 17.

I have broken so many cups in my house,

chipped the dishes,

cracks spread through ceramic like wildflowers.

The china is fragile – watch out – mend with gold – repair the shards,

glass lies broken on kitchen tiles (Sapphic and glittering).

I have run out of bandages,

the criss-cross scars of shattered crockery—

but that doesn't matter anymore.

Tangle with tea towels and cupboard doors,

I own so many mugs – so – that when the kettle boils we –

In my kitchen – can make tea.

Call me chamomile, mint.

My tablecloth stained sacred from spills

like a history project, amber with tea,

and it's raining outside so wipe steam from your glasses,

Complete the ritual,

and pour.

Stain me sacred – honey and ashes,

my garden is dripping with beehives and heather,

and I will change for the better,

head north.

Sadness is Black

By Niamh Langan, age 17.

So black your eyes can't see how black it is,

So black,

A black hole in the solar system, it sucks you in and you are gone forever.

Sadness is the headache from crying too hard

Without crying at all.

Sadness is the sick feeling in your stomach that has no reason to be there
but to damage.

Sadness is forgetting every plan and every goal

You have ever had,

Because you don't believe you're good enough to fulfil them,

You don't believe you'll even be around to live them.

Sadness is odourless like gas;

You don't know what it's doing to you until you breathe it in

Then you are lost and can't get out

It's too late and you drown.

Sadness tastes of nothing,

Yet is so strong it burns you from the inside out destroying every part of
you.

Sadness is black.

A silhouette of me.

A Cause

By Finn Doherty, age16.

I walk these streets alone

I'm just waiting for someone

To reap the seeds they've sown

To hand me a shotgun

And show me where to shoot

I need an absolute

I need a cause

Don't try to suppress me

Not bound by laws

Won't let you oppress me

I need a cause

They left us so guess we

We need a cause

I need a cause

We walk these streets at night

A switchblade in each coat

We're looking to start a fight

With some nearby scapegoat

Or someone not with us

We are really not that fussed

I've found a cause

We are doomed unless we

Fight these cruel laws

Won't let you oppress me

I've found a cause
Poor but nevertheless we
We've found a cause
I've found a cause
I walk these streets today
My battle scars still sting
Knee's about to give way
And my sore ears still ring
My little lad walks with me
And already I can see
He has no flaws
He just wants a cause

Corrupted

By Áine Winters, age 17.

I kept my hood up, shielding me from the relentless rain, as I hurried through the streets. Light was gradually fading, and the sunset adorned the puddles with gold. The streets were deserted, my footsteps the sole sound. Each stride echoed too loud for my liking. With my head down, my hood partially covered my face. It was dangerous to wander these streets at night, everyone knew that. But Mother had sent me to fetch her parcel regardless, deeming it precious enough to risk the perils. I made sure it was safely tucked into the folds of my jacket.

As the sun dipped below the horizon, bathing the world in a gentle darkness, I found myself at the centre of the town. The square, where public beheadings were held. Mother had never let me go to one, and a chill snaked its way down my spine simply from staring at that block. Nothing but a wooden boulder, carved to accommodate a human neck. Its groove had many chippings missing, where the axe struck. The blood was often cleaned from the pavestones, yet still they were tainted crimson from the rivers of blood that ran along them, often weekly. Town rumours claimed that if you listened closely to the wind, you could still hear the screams of those murdered upon the block. Shivering, I continued home.

I reached our driveway as the sky darkened to obsidian, the stars like spotlights in the dark. The redbrick walls loomed above me as I swung the gate open and strode across the short patch of grass we called a garden. I knocked on the door. Through the frosted glass, I saw a light flicker on, as a shadowed figure made its way down the hall to the door. The door clicked, before opening to reveal Mother. Her blonde hair hung limply from her head, as if she hadn't bothered to wash it lately. Swiftly ushering me inside, she ran a sharp, blue eye over me, examining for any sign of harm. Satisfied, she closed the door. I slowly took out the parcel, being careful not to rattle it. Whatever was inside, my mother had been willing to pay a lot of money for it. I didn't want it to break. Nodding her approval, she took the parcel from me.

'Thank you,' she mumbled, her face stony. Without saying another word, she carried the parcel into the kitchen, shutting the door in my face. Sighing, I peeled off the sodden coat and hung it up to dry. With a final glance at the door, perhaps expecting it to open, I trudged up the stairs to change into my nightclothes. Once I had completed that, I brushed my teeth and clambered into the freshly made bed. Before Papa had died, he would always tell me some story before I left for bed, no matter that I was too old for childhood fairy-tales. These nights, I often spent alone. My father's death had separated Mother and me, each communicating as little as possible to the other. I sighed, turning off my bedside lamp as I drew the covers up to my chin. Maybe in the morning, my mother would tell me what the parcel was.

Watery light shone through the translucent curtains, pulling me from the depths of my slumber. Quietly slipping out of bed, I shrugged on a light jacket to keep out the morning chill. The smell of cooking enticed me into the kitchen, where I found my mother standing by the stove. Sausages and eggs sizzled in the frying pans. She turned towards me, seeming more refreshed than she had in recent weeks. Her round face was devoid of the usual worry, and the fear in her eyes was replaced by something I dare call a sparkle of life. Her hair was freshly washed, styled in ringlets. Around her neck hung an emerald amulet. Cautiously, I shuffled over, taking a plate from the cupboard. While I piled my breakfast onto my plate, I eyed the amulet with distrust. I had never seen it before, and Mother rarely wore jewellery.

'Do you like it? It's to ward off the evil of magic.'

Magic. The word clanged through me. Only the most dangerous weapon anyone could have. Those in the town found guilty of possessing it were sent to the butchering block, no questions asked. There was no such thing as magic being used for good. Children were told bed time stories to keep them from staying up too late, about the magicians who would steal them away as slaves. Adults whispered about the times when magicians ruled the humans, trapping them through deception, trickery, and magic. Everyone had heard of the dark times, when magicians were free to do as they pleased with the helpless. It was in our nature to fear what we couldn't control. But we had our own reasons to despise the people cursed by a cruel twist of fate. Ever since Papa had died at the hands of a cruel, sadist magician, Mother had been searching for a way to keep the magicians far away from her. From me.

Pouring myself a cup of coffee, I took my usual place at the table. I tucked in to my loaded plate, pausing occasionally to sip from my mug. I took my time coming up with an answer.

'You know these things are often fake, Mother. The best protection you can have is your wits.' I watched as she slid into her own seat, opposite mine. She took a delicate bite of her breakfast, chewing slowly as she considered my advice. A small nod of her head was the only acknowledgement that she'd processed the information. Quickly devouring the rest of my own meal in silence, I stood and washed my plate. Once it was dried and set back into the cupboard, I made my way upstairs to get dressed.

Jeans, I had decided, were the most hated possession I owned. Struggling to pull them on, I hopped about on one foot, prancing about my room. After a long while of tugging and stumbling, they refused to slide on. Letting out a frustrated sigh, I kicked them off my legs. In doing so, my foot collided with the bedside drawer, and the lamp perched there wobbled. Yelping, I made to grab it, to hold it still. My fingers slipped. The lamp tumbled to the ground and shattered into smithereens. Cringing at the crash it made, I swore to myself. Mother was going to be furious. There was no way it could be pieced back together, or even partially glued. Staring at the shards of glass coating the bedroom floor, I listened to the quiet fall over the house.

'What was that?' my mother called to me, her tone wary.

'Nothing!'

I had kneeled down, wondering how on earth I was going to manage to pick it all up, let alone hide it, when it happened. The glass moved, pieces jumping from my hand and sliding onto the floor. Together they formed a neat pile beside the table, before rising and melding into a shape.

A fully formed, unbroken lamp.

I stared at the lamp, aghast. It simply wasn't possible. No magic ran in my veins. My parents were clean, and my grandparents, and my grandparents' parents. There had been no magic in my bloodline for centuries.

And yet the evidence was clear.

For several minutes, I sat there, gaping at what I had done. Too shocked to move, my limbs felt distant from my body, as if, spiritually, I was no longer there. A roaring silence filled my ears. The image of the broken lamp reconstructing itself played over in my mind, and yet I could not, would not, accept it. My heartbeat become a frenzy, pounding itself against my chest. I was not a magician. I wasn't to be killed upon that wooden block. That wasn't my fate. No. That fate belonged to another, someone dangerous, someone malicious. But not to me.

Only the sound of my mother's footsteps advancing upstairs dragged me out of my panicked thoughts. Hurriedly, I placed the lamp back in its proper position. The door handle clicked, and I involuntarily flinched. Blonde hair peeked through the crack in the door, before my mother opened the door wide enough to allow herself in. She scanned the room, looking for any evidence as to what the smashing may have been. But thanks to my newly discovered secret, there was none to be found.

'I was thinking we should take a walk, maybe around the park?' she suggested.

I blinked twice, trying to register her words. 'Sure.'

Mother smiled, a rare sight, and told me to get ready. The door closed once again as her head disappeared behind it. With a short sigh of relief, I sank onto the bed. I glared at the lamp, as if it was its fault I was an untrained magician, bound to be discovered and slaughtered. Of course, it didn't move. It stayed exactly where it was, as if mocking me. Growling, I pulled on my boots. How to deal with my magic was a problem for later. Right now, all I had to do was keep it hidden. It had, somehow, miraculously, stayed unnoticed for seventeen years. Surely it could stay that way for a few more hours.

She was waiting for me at the bottom of the stairs, her amulet still tucked around her neck. What would she do if she found out? Would she support me? Throw me out? Hand me over? Giving her a bleak, half-hearted smile, I pulled open the door. Cold blasted into my face with the force of a punch, and I stepped outside, relishing the damp wind on my skin. My boots crunched the frozen dew crystals on the grass. A deep breath filled my lungs with the biting chill of late winter air. As I tucked my hands into my pockets, my mother stepped to my side, turning to lock the door. Waiting, I stared down at my feet. Only to see the ice around me melting into water once more. I threw a swift glance at my mother, relief flooding my veins when her back stayed turned. Hastily stepping to the side, I turned away from it, hoping it would elude my mother's attention. With a cheery smile in my direction, she let go of the door handle and started down the driveway. I held my breath. She walked right past me.

And then past the melted crystals of ice.

My breath released itself from my chest in a whoosh of air, clouding before me. Setting my quaking legs into motion, I caught up with my mother, and walked alongside her. The silence settled in the space between us, and I attempted to slow my shaky breathing. Damp air clung to my hair, creating sparkling droplets. Snow sat in clumps at the bases of the trees lining our home street. The frigid temperature did nothing to stop my uncontrollable trembling. Beside me, my mother started humming a quiet melody to herself. We passed a group of children clowning around in the snow. Every family was outside together, enjoying the winter atmosphere. Kids shrieking as their parents chased them with snowballs in hand. Siblings teaming up to create snowmen. Entire families of snow angels lay on the front gardens of many houses. Once, the sight would have filled me with an urge to join in. Now, I had a new angle on the world. The children would likely run in fear if they knew who – what – I was. These neighbours, who played so innocently with their children, as if nothing was wrong, would turn me over to the authorities without hesitation. A lump formed in my throat. I turned away, repressing the sob that built in my chest. It was pointless thinking that way. Nothing could fix it anymore.

Mother turned to me, her cheeks flushed from the cold. A light dusting of snow glazed her hair, and the harsh winter light made her seem almost glowing. Timidly, she offered me a smile. This was as happy as I'd seen her since Papa's murder. Did having the amulet really make her feel secure enough not to worry? Maybe something else had changed, something she hadn't yet told me about.

'I've realised that in the past year or so...' She faltered, searching for her words. I waited. 'Maybe I haven't been the greatest mother to you. I should have talked to you more, done more with you. I'm sorry I didn't. I realised that...' Once again, her voice trailed off. Only this time, I could hear the emotion rising in her voice, the grief lingering in every word.

'That I never got to do a great deal of things I would have liked to with your father.'

Oh. Oh.

She continued, 'And I never will. But I shouldn't have let his death rip us apart as it did. This is not what he would have wanted, and I know that. So now, here, today, I want to start being a better mother for you. I want to be there, if you need me. Even if you don't! I just... I just want to let you know that you mean the world to me. Even when I don't show it.' Tears swelled in her eyes and dampened her lashes, threatening to overspill. She stared at me, and I realised she was waiting for my answer. I opened my mouth but found myself closing it again. I didn't trust myself to speak without letting her know what I was. To tell her to get as far away as possible from me. Instead, I wrapped my arms around her. And I started to bawl. Seconds later, I felt a warmth rest along my shoulders, pulling me into her embrace. I sniffed, taking in her faint scent of perfume and lavender. A hand ran over my hair as if it were made of delicate glass. For a moment, there was nothing else. Only the warmth of my mother's love and the sensation of being cherished again.

Gently detangling myself from her arms, I dried my red eyes. Upon looking up, Mother gave me a teary smile, and I gave a final sniff as we started our walk once more. Smiling, we wandered on. Snowflakes began to fall, each one glistening as it tumbled down from its cloud. Upon hitting the ground, they blended into their brethren, unable to be distinguished. At least, not unless you watched closely with a sharp eye. A surprised laugh burst from me, a sound I hadn't heard in a while. I grinned, catching a snowflake on my palm and watching it melt into nothing but a drop of water. Scurrying to keep up with my mother, I cradled the drop of water in my palm, until the cold had dried it up again. Everything was happening so normally. Nothing was out of order.

At least, not yet.

As we rounded the corner of the street to turn into the next, there was a sound of wheels crunching on ice. It happened too fast to register. One second, nothing was out of the ordinary. We were strolling along, minding our business. The next, there was the sound of wheels crunching on ice, and the skidding. Awful screeching of tyres, spinning to grip control that wasn't there to be had. Quicker than my eyes could process, the car was in front of us. The driver inside screaming, panicking. Twisting the wheel in a desperate attempt to avoid us. In a futile attempt. My muscles locked up, preparing for impact.

An impact that didn't happen.

My mind wasn't quick enough to react. But my magic was.

To both my relief and horror, the car slammed into an invisible wall directly in front of us. It halted too sudden for it to be anything else. Inside, the driver was thrown about like a rag doll. My chest caved in, before my heart began to pound thunderously. The car toppled onto its side from the force of hitting an object at such speed. People were staring now, some sprinting to help. My mother was staring at me, her hand clutched tightly around the necklace. She shouted something at me. Something I couldn't hear. There was a silence, such a loud silence drowning out everything else. My heart beat faster and faster with every eye that turned towards me. I had to get out of here. Even if I couldn't hear, I could see the word playing on their lips. Magician. Like a shushed whisper, rippling through the stunned crowd. They knew what I was, it was too late. I had to go, now.

Only my feet wouldn't move. My arms remained pinned to my sides. The tremors began to rack my body again. Adults rushed to help the driver and my mother. Some stayed back to call emergency services. Then there were people in front of me, hands on my arms, my shoulders, pushing me onto the ground. Grabbing me, holding onto me. I cried out in alarm.

Slowly, too slowly, I regained my senses. I could hear panicked yells, children screaming, babies crying. The pavement beneath me was cold, the loose stones were digging into my back. Fingers were squeezing my arms painfully tight, holding me still. Panic began to set in. I thrashed and struggled, to no avail. I screamed, kicked, wailed. They didn't care. I pleaded, for my life. They only tightened their grip.

They were going to kill me.

I had saved a life, and in return, they were taking mine.

I tried to tell them that it wasn't fair, that I was good. But there was no such thing as a good magician. Everyone knew that. My breaths were short, panicky. Sirens sounded off in the distance. Or maybe my ears were ringing. It was hard to tell. I arched my back, anything to get them to release their hold on me. Nothing worked. Somewhere to my left, there was a woman consoling my mother. My mother, who hadn't even tried to defend me. She knew I was good, she knew, she could tell them--

My arms were released. Aching, I sat up, rubbing at the red finger marks left behind. A new pair of hands grabbed me by the shoulders, shoving me back down to the ground. There was a sickening crack, and the world was black. The last thing I remember was the icy cold metal handcuffs biting into my wrists.

I came to in a bleak, grey prison cell. The handcuffs were still around my wrists, and around my ankles too. I wouldn't be getting anywhere very fast. I checked around, foolishly, for anything that might aid my escape. Nothing. Obviously. I felt the panic settle in again. There was no way out, no way to escape my fate. And they'd left me here to think upon it. To suffer. Sitting on the bed, the tears welled in my eyes. I hadn't asked for this, I never wanted to be a magician. I wasn't evil, I didn't want to hurt anyone. I just wanted to live. The tears overflowed, leaving warm, salty paths down my cheek. I continued to sit in a miserable silence. Nothing could be done. No one could save me. Now, I just wanted to die. Sitting there was torture.

After a while, the guards appeared at the cell door. Two of them, heavily armed. My body felt numb as they grabbed me and dragged me out of the cell. It couldn't be real, no, no, this wasn't how I died, was it? I struggled, weakly pulling away from their grip, but it was useless. Of course they were stronger than me. I felt the panic rising in my chest, the lump forming in my throat, the uncontainable hysteria spiralling out of my control. They yanked on the handcuffs, causing me to stumble, and when I regained my balance, we were facing a large, wooden door. The patterns and swirls carved into the door told me exactly where we were, confirmed my worst fear.

That door led directly to the square. The wooden block.

The door was pushed open. Warm, golden rays of sun shone upon my face, making me squint. My last sunset. Did Heaven have sunsets? Were magicians allowed in Heaven? What if even Hell didn't want me?! Where would I go?! The sob rose from my throat and I cried out, a desperate plea. But my eyes landed on the crowd gathered before me, and I knew it was hopeless to beg. They only cheered as the guards pushed me forward and four more circled me. I could see the wooden block, raised higher on a platform so all could watch. My stomach roiled at the red stones I would have to kneel upon. Soon, that would be all that was left of me. Dried blood on the cobblestones.

Surrounded by guards, I was forced to walk up the stairs. Each step I took rang through me like a death knell. Like my own death knell. My hands were visibly shaking. I couldn't hide. Forced onto my knees by the guards behind me, one of them placed a hand on the back of my head and shoved it into the groove. The marked, chipped groove. The crowd gathered at the bottom of the dais. My mother was among them somewhere. Frantically I scanned the crowd.

'Please, Mother!' I begged, my voice breaking with the effort of holding back my terrified tears.

My eyes met with hers. They no longer possessed the warmth they had held when she looked at me. Emotions were displayed across her face; fear, anger, betrayal. None of them kind. She made no acknowledgement that she'd heard me.

The headsman stepped up. Clothed in all black as per tradition, with his face hidden. In his hands he gripped his axe. It was polished and clean, a mockery of the invisible, already taken blood covering it. The guards surrounding me nodded, and he walked to my side, agonisingly slowly. He raised the blade above my head. Crying out in fear, the tears began to roll down my face in unstoppable rivers. Feebly raising my head once more, I looked to where my mother was standing. Still she clutched that amulet close. Still she believed I was a heathen. Her own flesh and blood. She raised her gaze to meet mine once more.

You're no child of mine.'

The words stung more than the blade as it cleaved through the air. Then through flesh and bone.

And my blood too, stained those pavestones red.

The Storyteller

By Annie Powell, age 16.

The journey across the page
An inanimate object made,
Animated.

Gliding, depicting a story,
An image of times gone by.
A blank canvas beautified
With the soft footsteps of
This storyteller.

The colours run down the page in
Complete coordination, so subtle,
Yet so bright
Creating a light, a spark of
True, pure times past…

No book, no voice, no song
Can tell a story quite like
The harrowing dance of
The storyteller.

Thánh Gióng

By Ben Martin, age 17.

The Vietnamese have many great heroes in their mythology. One in particular stood for the defeat of foreign invaders, and when the Americans came to wage war late in the 20th century, ancient and unsightly things that had lain waiting in the bloated and swollen jungle swamps rose once more-

Bangor, Maine, 30th of April 1978, five years after the end of the Vietnam War

'Mr. Moylan' said my psychiatrist, 'are you sure you're quite all right?'

I looked up. I had been staring out the thick glass window to my left and watching how the rain pattered softly against it, making a soothing noise that had completely distracted me. My psychiatrist, a pleasant woman with her hair tied back, sat across from me with her legs crossed, and was writing on the notepad she kept specifically for my appointments. It was considerably big at this point, I noticed. She asked me again, and I was finally taken enough away from my daydreaming to answer.

'Sorry, yes I'm fine thank you. Why do you ask?' I replied.

She looked at her notes before answering. 'You were about to tell me about a dream you've been having a lot lately. You said it was troubling you?' she said, and I remembered what we had been talking about. The dreams. I had said I wasn't really sure what to call it, as to the best of my knowledge I had been awake at the time, but dream seemed a suitable word for it.

'It was definitely troubling I'll say that,' I said, and I heard her pen scratching across paper once again. It was really quite irritating how loud it sounded, 'but I don't particularly want to talk about it thank you.' I smiled weakly, wanting to apologise but not really sure why.

I would love to tell her, but I feared she'd think I was mad, and I didn't want that. I might clench and unclench my hands when I was stressed, have a twitch in my trigger finger and jump with terror whenever I hear loud noises. I might become short of breath whenever I see violence on the television, and I might wake up drenched in cold sweat every morning, trembling. I might have done unspeakable things I now regret during the war. But one thing I was not was 'mad'. So, I kept my mouth shut and she accepted I didn't want to talk about it. Her pen continued to scratch and scribble loudly, and I decided I didn't like it. We small talked for another little while, all the time her pen whirring across the page. It really was loud, wasn't it? I couldn't stand it. Scratching and scrawling. My eye began to twitch, and the noise only intensified. The stress of that odd dream was getting to me I scolded myself. 'You should be much braver than this Moylan,' I told myself, 'You ran through the jungles of the underworld and came through but here you are whining about a little noise. Pathetic.' I began to sweat, and after another agonising few minutes I made my excuses and left, taking my fanciful tales of bad dreams with me out the door.

...

Driving home through the city streets, sky a clear blue and cool air floating in through the open window of my car after the rain had cleared up, I found myself again distracted and pondering the nature of those strange dreams. More importantly, mulling over why I had been so agitated. I had survived the Vietnam War for Christ's sake, and here I was only five years later struggling with daily life. People told me I was just finding it hard to readjust, but I couldn't for the life of me figure out why. Over in 'nam had been, for want of a better term, literal Hell. I had used my own friends as sandbags and spent weeks stumbling through that humid, muddy abyss, sharp thorns and leaves batting my skin, eyes wide with shellshock and exhaustion. Yet here I sat, traumatized by the mere though of ordering a coffee for fear that my hands might tremble so badly I spilt everything. This was something I thought often.

I came up to my house, sitting in Bangor's relatively peaceful outskirts, and pulled into the driveway. It was a nice place, a small bungalow with pastel blue boarding and flowerboxes in the windowsill, and a large back garden. The garden was my favourite place in the house, as I had filled it with flowers of all kinds and, at the very back behind two drooping, swaying willow trees, was a small stream that made soft bubbling noises as it rushed by, destined to join with the Penobscot at some point. I spent as much time out here as I could, sitting on the porch and being calm, no twitching or loud noises, only me and the water. I had originally hated it, as being so close to water brought back memories of the fallow, stinking swamp water I spent so much time wading through, screaming. But now those thoughts were gone, replaced by the whisper of the wind through the willow branches.

I walked in and closed the door, hanging up my coat and looking fondly at the framed picture of my squad from the war. The psychiatrist had suggested taking down memoirs, but I kept it up as a memorial to them. They were all dead now.

...

I sat on the porch outside and enjoyed the sunshine, listening to the calming sounds surrounding me. My neighbours had given a cheerful 'Hey there Mr. Moylan,' when they saw me from across the fence, and I had waved back at them before returning to my thoughts. It had been a busy year so far, what with the Soviets acting up yet again and the Middle East quickly becoming a brawling pit, but I was glad to be observing from a distance. Here in my small little corner of Maine I could sit and watch the world go by without having to be one of the poor suckers on the front lines. I looked up and realised my neighbour had been calling me from over the fence. My hearing had been shattered in the war and I apologised to the neighbour before asking what he wanted on this fine day sir. 'Jus' checking in on you, you looked mighty dreadful there,' he said. I was surprised and told him I was fine before he disappeared again. Had I been looking sad? I hadn't realised at all. Maybe that whole psychiatry business had me all shook up I thought to myself, and I decided to have a nap.

Waking up, I realised it was much later than I anticipated, and I quickly made myself a small meal before heading to my desk. I had become fond of writing down my thoughts lately, despite the fact nobody but me will ever read them. I had filled the entirety of my first journal only two days ago, and I was already nineteen pages into my newest one. Admittedly this one was far less helpful, as I dreaded flicking through it to see where I had left off. During this journal, and the latter half of the last one, the dreams had started. As I sat down and wrote, my focus sadly went back to them, drawn like a moth to a lamp, not knowing it would burn me. They had begun on the anniversary of my squad's death, some months ago, and only seemed to be getting worse.

The dreams were a curious thing, happening once every month or so. I did insist they were dreams, it was the only way I could keep myself sane after all, for if they weren't dreams then what were they? I called them dreams because they couldn't possibly be real, yet they did not happen when I was asleep, and seemed to bend seamlessly into reality like a daydream. One minute everything was normal, the next that stinking, brackish water was covering the floor and... they were there. The first appeared through my walls, chasing me and screaming of sins I would rather forget. The second had climbed out of the refrigerator, twisting itself in uncanny ways while a torrent of water poured from inside behind it, splashing everywhere. Each came, and each told me all sorts of terrifying things. The first psychologist I went to had suggested it was some kind of extreme reaction to the anniversary, the second psychologist had told me it was severe PTSD. I had believed the first one's advice until the second dream, where I realised his symptoms did not match. That time I had been prepared, and had waded through the water to my bedroom, where I grabbed my Browning Hi-Power from under my pillow and unloaded it into that... abomination. Which, to my surprise, worked, at least until the bullets ran out. The second psychologist gave me sleeping pills, but these did not work and only gave me more nightmares, though of a more mundane sort. Now I simply went to a normal psychiatrist to talk about, well, anything other than those dreadful waking dreams.

The last one had been yesterday, but I had a feeling the giant boy had more on its mind for me than just hauntings, and as dusk crawled closer I grew more fearful by the second.

···

The sun sank down, colour spilling across the sky like a sanguine curtain, before it disappeared completely below the horizon and the sky was filled with flickering stars. Crickets chirped out by the stream and I sat on my sofa watching the newsreel. Some other Soviet scandal, no surprises there, with President Carter trying his best to clear up the mess. At least the world was calmer, no less than a decade ago the threat of imminent death hung over everybody like a shroud, and I applied for the armed forces because I wanted to stop that. In the end all that had happened was that we had caused more misery than there had been when we began.

I stretched and got up to head to bed. At this point I was worn out after the long day and headed to the bathroom, showered and brushed my teeth and took my sleeping pills, and then went to my bedroom. I crawled into bed and, hand wrapped around the comforting handgun under my pillow, attempted to fall asleep. Then, just as I thought I was about to fall into a dreamless sleep, I heard it. The faint echoes of gunfire, bouncing down the hallway towards my room. Jolting violently up into a sitting position, I saw the lights outside my bedroom flickering, and felt the air become steadily more humid and sickly as the faint sounds of splashing water and the shrieks of dying men slowly grew in pitch.

It was starting again. The 'dreams'.

...

'Mr Moylan', I told myself, 'just sit back down and ignore it. Ignore the screams and the water that, should you step off your bed, would surely be there. Just ignore it. It's all in your head. You know what you did and God is punishing you for it you pathetic-'

My thoughts were interrupted by the realisation that this was one dream too many. I did not have any squad-mates left, they had all visited to torment me each other dream, one by one, and so what would happen in this one? Would the giant boy himself visit me?

I reached under my pillow and grasped my gun tightly, the Browning's powerful weight a welcome reassurance in my grip. I slid quietly off the bed, and sure enough my feet landed in a thin layer of warm, fallow water. It was covered in algae and moss, which clung to my ankles and made anything other than a slow walk treacherous at best. I started forward and slowly opened my door. Out here the lights flickered manically, and a vile stench wafted from the living area, a stench of melting, cooking meat and burning vegetation. Eventually, with my gun's ugly muzzle pointed straight ahead, I entered my living area and I was greeted with yet more water. The room was at a lower level than my hallway, and although the indent was only a foot deeper, the water appeared black and endlessly deep. Strange shadows flowed across the walls, reminding me of some crooked malevolent forest. This was usually where they appeared to me, my dead comrades, where they taunted me and spoke to me in their harrowing whispers of the things that I have done. But now, they did not manifest, but I strangely felt that I needed to go outside. Why I felt this I don't know, but I was compelled to wade through the deeper water to reach my back door. It reached my waist, impossibly, and beneath the water I felt muddy soil and broken branches, a waterlogged forest floor. Bullet casings lay amidst the moss, I felt them cold against my bare feet, and it took me seemingly an age to reach the door.

Heaving myself out of the stagnant water and opening the door, I staggered out into my garden, normally so calm and peaceful. The flickering of the lights followed me, reminding me once more of gunfire, and the sounds of war were so loud out here I had to cover my ears. The song of violence ripped through the air, ratatatat, and at this point I was too afraid to even cry out.

Just as I was about to find my voice I saw it, and a scream caught in my throat like a bullet lodged in a wound. Behind the garden, behind my peaceful little stream, the Vietnamese jungle spread out in all its horrid glory, framed by the willow branches so at odds with the sickening vibrant green and shadowy dark. I could see shapes moving through the rainforest, running and shouting orders. Then, the water in the stream went still and dark also, and a hand reached up from its depths, dragging my very worst nightmares with it.

The form that pulled itself up into my garden was not natural. A skeletal, ragged thing, covered in torn shreds of cloth and dripping red, it stood askew. It was a corpse, almost midnight black with charred and burned flesh, with the skin on its face pulled back to reveal a twisted grin. Its leg was bent in the wrong places, and I knew with dreadful certainty that this was Coleman, my best friend during the war. Behind him the water bubbled and bulged and more figures began to emerge, one by one. Patterson, now a stick-thin monstrosity, rotting and decayed with a bullet hole in his forehead. One, surrounded by a halo of blue and ghostly flame, writhing as though it could still feel the napalm's impossible heat, was Legrasse, and he stumbled forth on bony legs to stand beside his compatriots. O'Brian and the rusted remains of his autogun came next, his chest cavity opened up to reveal all his grisly insides. And finally Samuel, the youngest of the squad and almost like a son to me. I could see the bullet holes that riddled him even from here, and instead of screaming I began to weep. Why was this happening to me, why?

Deep inside I knew why, and the giant boy knew too. They were soot-stained and black from fires lit by me, the 'miraculous' lone survivor of an unnamed assault, on that all too fateful day.

...

And there, behind my stream on the banks of the jungle, it stood. Atop a horse made of beaten iron, its insides glowing with heat, was the entity that I witnessed all those years ago as I ran, lost, through the rainforest. I had only seen him just for a second, out of the very corner of my eye, but it was enough. Its impossibility had sent me mad, and in a rage I had done... unspeakable things. And when I recovered my senses I could do nothing but return to base at Lai Khe and lie, and lie and lie and lie for the past five years. A giant creature, which my mind for reasons unknown referred to as simply a 'boy', a scared and crying boy alone after a devastating war, sat across from me. Its skin, like the malignant and ghastly apparitions it had created, was burnt, and encased in its ornate armour it wielded rods for whipping. Somehow, despite its appearance it seemed to look entirely natural within the confines of the thick jungle, like it could belong nowhere else in the world, and as I watched it lowered the rod and simply pointed at me. The dead surged forward and grabbed me, their skin like dough and sharp bones digging into me, and began to drag me towards the jungle at the end of my garden. I did not resist, and accepted my fate almost gladly, crying. The walking cadavers of my friends at once began speaking in their rasping wet voices, whispering of what I did.

...

They told the story of how, in my anger, I had killed them, and when I came back to my senses I had burned their bodies in napalm and simply walked away.

And the giant boy, ancient and archaic as it was, simply watched as it did its duty.

Magpie

By Anna Gillespie, age 16.

Sorrow, she knew the word well,
Drifting from the lips of passers by
Some would hastily avert their gaze
As if she wasn't there, but she never knew why
Others though, would acknowledge her presence
With a wave, or salute, or a simple nod of their head
At moments like that, for some strange reason
Her day was filled with a little less dread.

Sorrow, it seemed her only label now
It was all that people knew of her, all that they could see
'That can't be all I am,' she thought,
'There must be more that I can be.'
In the distance she saw another,
Someone as confused and lonely as she
'Maybe,' she thought, 'they feel the same sadness,
The same sadness that lives inside me.'

Sorrow, she noticed it in them now,
They didn't need to have tears streaming from their eyes
Because you see, the ones who feel the most pain
Need not be the ones who always cry.
She thought she should speak to them,
To say they are not alone

In feeling the weight of sadness
But knowing it can never be shown.

She hated living feeling no one understood
Never wanting to confide, in fear that she'd annoy
But seeing someone like her, she felt there was hope
If two sorrows were no longer alone, maybe they'd be joy
She now felt she had an answer
In her mind and heart she knew
She spread her white and black wings wide
And in a blur of feathers she flew.

Undead City

By Freyja Hellebust, age 17.

It's a warm evening, and the metal of the chairs outside the bar is pleasant against the skin.

Cigarette smoke and idle chatter mingle in the open air of the ancient stone square, unchanging, imperial, cosmopolitan.

The place is still bathed in sunlight, but the soft kind, and some of the restaurants will begin turning on the fairy lights hanging around the smoking areas.

Young girls in crop tops and shorts sit around, legs crossed, casual and oh so cool.

Impossibly beautiful boys flirt with them, everyone oozing effortless perfection. Cherry lip-gloss stains the glasses that once contained dainty, peachy drinks.

The cobblestones are smooth and shiny. A beach, the one nearest to the city, is a sandy strip lined with sparkling turquoise. It is slightly less populated, but there are still plenty of sun-kissed swimmers, lying contented on beach towels.

Music plays from various speakers, the listeners whooping with the joy of youth, of beauty, of the knowledge that they are together and they are the best.

A group of children gone feral roam around, yelling. One struggles with an ice cream that is melting faster than she can eat it.

The scene, centuries old, feels like freedom, like being somebody else.

In this paradise of palm-tree Tropicana, the dead are coming back to life.

They're not quite temporal enough to really manage, but they amble through the golden world as best they can, wanting to catch a taste of the warmth they have lacked for so long.

A senator leans against a stone arch he remembers as new, and watches people as they stroll by, heavy make-up and light words.

'I'd like one of those,' he sighs, nodding wistfully at a box of cigarettes. It is set down on the wall alongside a pair of sunglasses. The couple they belong to are leaning on each other, deep in conversation.

He thinks he could probably swipe them.

He leans over, emitting a slight chill, and grabs them both.

He slips the glasses on, grins, and sticks a cigarette between his teeth. When it doesn't immediately light up, he puzzles over it for a few minutes, before clicking his fingers dramatically.

The end of the cigarette is suddenly alight, and he puffs away happily.

An 18th-century noblewoman makes her way over to him. She is smirking coquettishly and sipping a pink lemonade. She doesn't want to be drunk. She wants to remember this.

This attitude is not shared by all. In what were once dusky taverns, the resurrected are ordering countless drinks. This is good for business, and superstition is pushed aside. The realisation that the dead are penniless will not hit until tomorrow.

They congregate, united by a mutual understanding, a wonder at how the world has changed.

By the time the star-studded curtains of night are drawn, they are everywhere, milling around excitedly.

The night, ironically, is alive.

The dead decide to go swimming.

The beach is truly empty now, everyone enticed away by the gaudiness of the city in the dark, and there is nobody around to witness the not-quite-ghosts as they wade into the sea.

The dark blue water is startlingly cold compared to earlier, but it is still pleasant. They don't really mind anyway, their still blood chilled by an eternity spent underground.

The senator has finished his fags, and now stands up to his waist in water, giggling uncontrollably, sunglasses still on.

The sternness of the crypt, a leftover from life, has been eroded throughout the day until there is nothing left but the urge to live, to smile.

He is hand in hand with the noblewoman, who has decided that if the modern girls wear next to nothing, why should she bother with corsets.

They throw each other into the waves with wild abandon.

John Keats is nearby, serenely doing the backstroke fully clothed.

A woman has draped herself over a sunbathing chair, reminiscent of a smaller Angel of Grief, just as cold and grey.

Someone has got their clammy hands on a rickety violin and is drawing out a tune to which a few people are swaying, a true danse macabre.

The senator, who has decided he is an emperor, carries his empress around the soft blue beach.

Her long hair is too heavy for the gentle breeze, weighed down as it is by seawater and sand. Tendrils of it are tangled everywhere, but neither of them mind.

She has never felt this free.

The living are not sure why they are reluctant to go near the beach. It's a glitch in their vision, too hard to concentrate on. Nobody thinks about it too much, their minds feeling vaguely fuzzy.

But the opaque veil between the worlds has been lifted tonight, something in the sunset reversing the irreversible.

Nobody wants to ever leave the beach, but the emperor and the empress, the night being still young, decide to explore what has once been their city. There is a bitter sweet excitement when a monument is recognised, some familiar landmark amid swathes of alien newness.

It is overwhelming for the emperor, who had privately prided himself on being quite stoic, and he oohs and aahs at everything.

The empress laughs at him, baring her pearly teeth.

They are both barefoot now, and feel the soaked-up warmth of the ground. They grin at each other, eyes glowing.

A young boy is staring at them, mouth open.

'Are you God?' he asks the emperor.

The great man, who could once have passed for divine, who believed his people to be descended from gods, currently gives the impression of a stag night gone wrong, or, debatably, right.

He bends down and pats the boy on the shoulder.

'Yes,' he says in the voice he used to reserve for politics. He straightens up, opens his arms wide. 'Spread the message,' he booms. The empress is in fits of laughter.

The child stares at them both, drenched, manic, dressed as though straight from the circus.

He runs and spends the rest of his life wishing he hadn't.

When dawn breaks, it does so cheerily, pale pink and bright light, hours later than all the bakeries.

The pigeons flap around in droves, cooing and warbling contentedly.

Once more, the streets are walked by the living, busy, beautiful, immortal in the not yet scorching sunlight.

The dead relinquish their nocturnal kingdom, and trudge dutifully back to their final resting places.

Something feels fresher, lighter, and they settle back into the ground to await the next party.

Aftermath

By Eileen Cloonan, age 17.

I remember the
Fire that caught in
The sheets when
I was with you.
You were the
Flame that
Replaced my cigarettes, but
Now smoke replaces you again.
I remember the days
Before they
Filled my lungs, those
Days you filled my
Heart with, and
Empty space didn't
Exist anymore.

Exploring in the
Abandoned and lonely, the
Houses and our bodies;
Tastes and temperatures and
Our fingertips froze time. In a
Peaceful February
We paced fast, and
Traced our
Edges intertwined.

I remember the two dogs that
Followed and
Coveted our attention, their
Paws magnetic to our
Footprints in the dirt and their
Breaths a homely fireplace.
They were the fires we
Needed in our
Makeshift squats
Who kept the wind from
Invading through the
Holes in our
Trespassing shoes.

Then hell rose
Through the cracks in
Our friendship, and
Broke apart the
Roots that
Stabilised our time.
Now you've no motive to
Move closer again because
Time and bitterness is
Distancing the
Platforms where we stand.

You remind me of an apple
Falling from a tree,
The way you fell from me. I'm sorry I

Scratched you as you
Hung from my branch and the
Way my words
Pecked and you swayed.
I didn't realise
What I'd lost until
Fire and grounded hatred
pushed you away.

A Queen's Curse

By Caoimhe Rudden, age 17.

Queen Calista of Vaceris had an impeccable memory. Many would call this a blessing. She disagreed. She could remember so many things; things a part of her begged the rest of her to forget. Names, the faces that went with those names, the names whispered by the owners of those names and faces as they heaved their final breaths. The faces of the bereaved. The many faces worn by those that stalked her court.

The smallest things could bring a memory to haunt her. The crisp air of a spring morning. The way the dew settled on the grass. The way motes of dust fell softly in a beam of light. Tonight it was the scent of the damp logs smoking on the fire that carried memories to her, the acrid smoke tinted with the faint smell of pine that stuck in the back of her throat: it reminded her of her brother and the events leading up to his death.

She woke from the nightmare with a start – heart pounding in her chest, forehead slick with sweat. Dapples of moonlight peeked through her curtains as she rose from her bed. This distorted memory had been continuously haunting her for a while. Now she mulled it over in her mind. She sat in a wooden chair with intricate dragon carvings on the armrests by the hearth in her chambers, staring at the smoking logs. Her heavy fur-lined cloak drowned her body, protecting her from the winter chill. Wine filled a silver goblet held loosely in her hand, all but forgotten as she stared broodingly at the flames that crackled and spat at her from the hearth.

The day Claude had strolled into her chamber to find her perched on her desk was when it had all began. She had tensed immediately upon hearing his laugh outside the door as he joked with a guard. He didn't bother to knock.

'Ho there, sister.'

She slowly looked up and pushed herself from the desk, tucking the letter under a pile of missives.

'Have you completely abandoned your manners?' she snapped, examining his gait as he approached: his head was held high and he puffed out his chest as he unclipped his gauntlet. The spurs on his boots made a distinctive clink as he walked.

'Hmm? I don't know what you mean,' he peered down at the sheets on the table, picking one up. 'Anything interesting in these?'

Calista had rounded the table in a second, snatched the missive from his hand and for a moment she allowed rage to flicker on her features before she caught herself.

Claude raised an eyebrow and the corner of his mouth twitched.

'Don't touch those,' she sighed, turning to place the sheet back on the small pile, 'I just organised them and I shan't do it again because of your meddling.'

'They don't look very organised to me.'

She watched him thumbing at a few missives, getting too close to her letter. She wasn't ready to confront him yet, and chose to drive him away instead.

'I am not in the mood for your antics today, Claude. Either heed me or get out.'

...

He chuckled, 'Be at ease, Cal,' he patted her shoulder, 'No need to get prickly.'

A swat of her hand quickly removed his from her shoulder and she took a defensive step forward, 'Do not forget yourself,' she warned. 'Leave me.'

He took a step back and rolled his eyes, not meeting her gaze as he crossed the expanse of the room, slightly less confident than before and pulled the door closed as he left. She heard the guards laugh again.

The queen exhaled shakily, grabbing the documents and stomping back around the table to the window, so close that her breath appeared as condensation on the glass, lip trembling and eyes watering with a mixture of rage and disbelief.

How he could be so brash was beyond her. He was not a child anymore. Neither of them were. She had a hard time accepting this, especially when the letter had been delivered to her hands that morning.

This letter had held details of Claude's recent exploits and details of his imminent betrayal.

'Blood means nothing in this game,' her dead father's voice echoed in her mind and she shivered at the thought of King Gailan; he had been the definition of iron fisted during his rule.

Claude was a complication, a wound that festered, but how could she seek a cure? He was her little brother, after all.

'You would be a fool to allow this to continue,' the dead king hissed in her mind, 'Did I leave my throne to a fool Queen?'

She had then hurled the parchments in rage, watching as they floated to the ground nearby.

She remembered how once, during a visit to the marketplace, some of the local boys teased Claude. She was no older than thirteen and he merely nine years of age and these boys had towered over her, but she had placed her hands on her hips and strode towards them with all the confidence in the world.

'Leave my brother alone!' she snapped, with Claude cowering behind her.

'Who are you to tell me what to do?' one had chortled, poking his finger to her shoulder repetitively.

Calista had grabbed his finger and pushed it backwards, too quickly for him or his friends to comprehend.

'When I am queen,' she hissed, bending his finger back so far that she had him on his knees, 'I'll have you skinned and boiled, you rat!'

She remembered the satisfying crack as his finger broke, and how he and his friends had screamed. The adults had come running. Out of the public eye, her father had praised her. He sent Claude to his room for being such a coward. Calista snuck into his room later that night to check on him.

'Thank you for stopping them, Cal,' he whispered as she drew him towards her for a hug.

'I'll always defend you, don't fret,' she replied, beaming at him with pride, 'there's no need to worry when your big sister is around.'

...

Within weeks of receiving the letter, whispers of rebellion had reached her. She needed to act, but who could she trust?

'Nobody,' whispered the dead king, 'If you cannot trust your own flesh and blood, how can you trust anyone?'

She remembered the evening, not long after her sixteenth birthday when her father made her watch as he executed Gareth. She had been standing not far away, having retreated to the other side of the table when her cousin had been summoned.

'You dare test me. You dare to adhere to my enemies?' her father was not a man known to raise his voice. He was terrifyingly calm, his voice low and steady, but laced with venom.

This General – Gareth – was a cousin of her father's. She had grown up around this man, he was family. She remembered the small embellished dagger he always had on his person. She remembered how smooth the hilt had been the day he had allowed her to hold it, the small emeralds embedded in it glinting in the sunlight, the smell of freshly cut grass around them as the stood in the gardens.

King Gailan had drawn his sword without hesitation and she remembered Gareth begging for mercy that he would never receive. She remembered how it had taken her father two swings to fully decapitate him and how his blood on the floor made her gag and turn away. Her father had terrified her in that moment.

She heard him take slow steps towards her trembling form.

'Turn around, Calista. Turn and look.'

'I can't,' she whispered. 'The blood...'

'Do not be afraid of blood,' he placed a calloused hand on her shoulder and spun her to face him. He smelled of pine and mead, but the sharp metallic scent of blood overpowered that. 'It is our duty to eliminate any threats to our kingdom. Someday the time will come where you will have to spill blood too.'

She remembered how he had dragged her over to the body, despite how she resisted. Gareth's eyes were glazed over and rolling in his head, which had fallen not far away. She felt bile rise in her throat at the sight, but swallowed it down.

'Take his dagger.' The King's voice had startled her. 'Take the dagger and plunge it into his chest.'

'He's already dead, Father,' she whispered, fixing her gaze on the floor not too far away, 'I don't need to—'

Her father bent down and grabbed the dagger from Gareth's belt before holding it out to his daughter. 'Do as I say.'

She took the dagger from him and slowly looked down at the corpse. Blood that had pooled on the floor was soaking through the hem of her dress, permanently staining the material. She could feel it on her feet too: her slippers too thin to prevent it. She gagged. She felt her father position the dagger in her hands – it was as smooth as the first time she held it.

Her father bent down and prodded at Gareth's chest.

'Here, here is where his heart is. That is your target.'

She raised the dagger above her head and she remembered how in her mind she was shouting at herself, 'This is wrong! He's already dead!' but she dared not defy her father.

The blade met flesh. It was softer than she had expected and she found herself twisting the knife upon contact with a rib. She remembered stumbling forward as the bone broke, sending her onto her knees. Calista cringed as she heard a squelch and she let go of the knife, raising her hands, unsure where to place them. Her eyes filled with tears and she shut them tight

She remembered her father pulling her to her feet, the feeling of his thumb smearing blood across her cheeks. She held her breath, trying to avoid inhaling the execrable scent.

'Open your eyes, Calista,' the King ordered.

She opened her eyes, allowing tears to roll freely down her cheeks, mixing with the blood already there.

'Queens do not cry. Dry your tears.'

She did as she was told and scrubbed at her face with her sleeves, further rubbing the blood into her skin. She tried to ignore how her powder-blue dress was now red.

Her father grabbed her hand and placed the dagger in it.

'That is yours now. Do with it as you wish.'

With that he turned on his heel and left the room, leaving Calista to empty the contents of her stomach in the corner.

'I cannot trust even those closest to me,' she muttered to herself one night in her chambers, glancing towards her father's sword mounted on the wall.

'You will know what to do when the time comes,' the dead king rested a hand on her shoulder, a small touch of affection that was too good to be true, for when she turned around he was gone, a ghost once more.

She remembered the scrabbling of Claude's boots against the polished tiles in the throne room as the guards dragged him away to the dungeons. The sound of his golden spurs scratching the ground made her cringe.

'You can't do this to me,' he seethed, attempting to resist. 'You have no proof! You're insane.'

She remembered the sound of his spurs clinking as he stalked the shadows of her room three nights later. He thought she hadn't heard him enter. How had he escaped the dungeons? How had he gotten in?

The guards, she thought, the guards are dead.

'Or they'll wish they were,' the King's voice encouraged her from the depths of her mind, 'But first you must deal with the problem at hand...'

She clutched the dagger in her hand under the covers and adrenaline flooded her system. She wanted to run, but she couldn't. She heard him pull her father's sword from the display on the wall.

'I came to kill you...' he slurred and it was then that the smell of alcohol met her.

'With any hope,' she thought, 'He'll swing and miss.'

He sat on the edge of her bed and passed the sword from one hand to the other. 'I don't really want to kill you,' he mumbled.

'Strike now! Show him no mercy!' Her father's orders echoed in her mind.

She remembered the shock on his face when she lunged for him, blade catching his cheek. He stood in panic and dropped the sword, clutching his wound.

Calista was up in an instant, knowing that if she allowed him to recover she would never win. He was not so little anymore. She could not overpower him.

She grabbed her father's sword from the floor and discarded the dagger. She remembered how the flames of the hearth danced across the blade as she swung it with no apprehension. He attempted to back away, but he was not quick enough in his intoxicated state and she embedded the blade in his arm, tearing the muscles. He screamed and stumbled onto the floor, clutching his wound.

'Don't do this!' he had sobbed. 'You're becoming so much like father!'

Calista did not change her expression. She would not give him that. 'Good!' she had replied, as she raised the sword above her head.

She remembered crunch as the blade broke his ribs, piercing his heart and cringed at the familiarity of the noise and the terrible smell of blood that assaulted her senses.

Nausea clawed at her throat and she abandoned the sword, turning away as she tried to control her reflex, but it was too late and the bile fought its way up her throat. She lurched forward and fell to her knees, face pale and dripping with sweat and tears. Despite emptying her stomach, all Calista could smell were the damp logs smoking in the hearth.

Tonight's nightmare had involved Claude rising up from his place on the floor, pulling the bloodied sword from his chest before swinging at her, the cut on his cheek revealing his jawbone and teeth.

She knew it was a nightmare of course, she remembered how he looked the last time she seen him. 'Unfortunately,' she would add. She hadn't sliced his cheek that deep.

The Queen knocked back the last of her wine and abandoned the goblet once she had finished musing to herself.

She rose and stretched, hearing the satisfying pop of her shoulders, which had never quite recovered from her over-exertion the night she had killed Claude.

Calista draped the robe on the end of her bed before tucking herself in tightly under her mountain of covers. The smell of lavender found her and she shut her eyes, remembering the afternoon her family had spent picnicking in a field full of the plant, before everything had changed.

Two Children

By Anna O'Callaghan, age 17.

Two children of the night,
Darkened souls weaved with pinpricks of light.

Two children of the sea,
Dragged to shadowed depths
That the lighthouse cannot reach.
Never saved,
No one hears their pleas.
Those dying whispers carried on the ocean's empty breeze.

Once children of the sun,
Achingly soft and light and young.
Crowned by love and light,
'Til hate and darkness won.
Then they came and stole their light,
Weapons trained on anything that shone.
These children,
Whose hearts once burned so bright,
Now nothing more than dying embers in the night.

Sarah's Friend

By Catherine Gallagher, age17.

For as long as I could remember, I had always just been 'Sarah's Friend'. Not that I minded or anything, honestly. There's nothing else in the whole wide world I would have rather been than 'Sarah's friend'. Of course I was ONLY 'Sarah's friend'. When she tried introducing me to her parents, they had laughed at her and patted her mop of sandy curls, looking straight past me as they said 'Hello!' and gave each knowing smiles. I could never understand why 'Hello' was the only thing anyone said to me. If they wanted to know my age, or even how I looked (which I found quite rude considering I was standing right in front of them most of the time), they would ask Sarah, who would babble off my appearance to them happily. The way those adults would whisper to one another after Sarah and I had returned to our games made me uneasy. How could anyone say a bad word against her? She was the most precious girl in the entire world! I couldn't help but think she was absolutely spectacular. When she smiled at me with those eyes filled with thunder and lightning and rain, I felt like I could accomplish anything.

Then...things changed...

Sarah began to grow up. No longer was she a fearless four-year-old. The weeks had turned to months and the months had changed to years. Sarah was now six years old. I could hardly believe it. Time seemed to fly when I was with her. Now, rather than spending our time playing all day in her room or in her yard, we would rush out in the morning to catch the school bus and learn tons of things in her school. She would take me with her to all of her playdates, and we'd spend hours working on her maths homework, which neither of us had a clue on how to finish. I couldn't help but notice just how much she had changed. Somewhere along the line she'd taken a notion to chop off her long golden locks and now rocked a long-bob better than anyone! Of course it suited her, because everything did. Every few months she would flash me these wide gaps in her gums where her teeth had fallen hostage to the tooth fairy. I would always tease her for getting old and tell her to try and enjoy being little just a little more than she was. It always flew over her head though… Oh, how I wished and wished that she would have listened to me. I never seemed to change like Sarah did. In fact, I remained very much the same as I had always been. Sarah was changing everyday, growing up and finding her place out in the world. It...scared me... And I could never figure out just why it did.

Seven years old. My, she was absolutely beautiful. Her smile made the stars jealous with its radiance. Where had the time gone? My beautiful girl was almost all grown up! I loved telling her that and doting on her from time to time, but for some odd reason, she wasn't always able to...hear me. It was probably my fault for not speaking loudly enough. She would look dazed for a moment, like she'd lost something, or forgotten something important and then giggle like she knew something I didn't before resuming her game. Sarah knowing something I didn't, made me feel so...uncomfortable, because Sarah told me everything. I tried talking to her parents about it, but they were too busy to really pay any attention to me then, so I left it alone. Our friend, Pauline, who sat beside Sarah at school, would come over to play almost every day too, but she was just like Sarah's parents in a way. Like, when they'd try and think of something to do together, Sarah would suggest a 'three-person-or-more' game and Pauline would laugh at her and say something along the lines of, 'With only two people?' and then I would interrupt and remind them that they did in fact have more than two people and that they could play whatever they wanted, but then they would always just end up agreeing to play hopscotch or something like that and I would sit and watch because I'd somehow convinced myself that I now one, hated hopscotch and two, hated Pauline and would have preferred to watch them giggle and laugh.

With every day that passed, I began to notice just how clearly I could see the girls when I hid my head in my knees. I could almost see completely through them now, which I found strange. It was like patches of them had just...vanished. I would use the excuse, 'I'm feeling weak', which wasn't a complete lie. I felt...strange. Less 'in touch' I suppose. I tried to tell Sarah about it on the night of her eighth birthday, but she must have already fallen asleep because she never responded to me...

As the weeks and months ticked on, Sarah spoke to me less and less and for the longest time, I could not figure out why. I just couldn't understand what I had done wrong, and it made me feel so distraught. I never yelled at Sarah but now sometimes I had to if I wanted her to hear me. Sometimes, it was like she wasn't able to hear me at all. I would say something and her eyes would just glaze over slightly before she would resume whatever it was that she was doing... but how ridiculous did that sound? Sarah and I were best friends. I understood most things about her, but this? I didn't understand any of this until she turned ten years old.

And then, everything clicked.

Why she wasn't responding to me anymore. Why her parents never seemed to want to talk to me. Why Sarah had always been the only one to ever directly address me, I knew.

I wasn't afraid when I realised ,wasn't even shocked really. A part of me deep down had known all along – that this was how it was meant to be. I guess that part of me just didn't really want to believe it. I had completed my duty to Sarah, and served my purpose and now... it was my time to go.

The night it happened was cold. Wind whispered softly through the cracks in Sarah's window. Snow was falling outside, causing their shadows to dance across the floor gracefully as they tumbled to the ground. She was sleeping peacefully, snoring softly like she always did when she slept on her side. I still remember how she looked. Not a care in the whole wide world.

It was difficult to get close to her. I'm practically non-existent now, even more so than I already was. My skin and clothes are completely transparent, and when I catch myself in Sarah's mirror, I'm just able to make out my outline. I somehow, however, manage to perch myself on the edge of my girl's bed, feeling thick, warm tears begin to crawl down my cheeks. I smile softly, leaning down to press a soft kiss to her forehead, before settling down to lie beside her and watch her sleep peacefully. 'Goodnight Sarah.'

I feel a tugging in my very soul and I shakily exhale, feeling the last ounce of strength sap from my body. Just as everything goes dark, I manage to whisper a soft, 'Goodbye' and then...

There's nothing.

Nothing at all.

The next morning, Sarah woke up like nothing had changed, and after washing and dressing, happily skipped down the stairs to breakfast, kissing her mother and father both as she always had done. This morning seemed just the same as any other. That was until her mother asked her a peculiar question that confused her for the rest of the day. 'What ever happened to that friend of yours...uh...Charlie, I think her name was?'

Sarah squinted at her mother, puzzled as she wracked her brain. 'Charlie?'

'Wasn't she your imaginary friend?' her mother said again and Sarah shrugged, the name not ringing a bell. Her mother and father seemed to give each other a knowing look before her mother brushed off the question and rushed her out the door to school. However later that evening, after Sarah had returned from school and gone up to bed again for the night, her mother stepped outside, breath rising in the cold air and smiled up at the twinkling stars above their little town.

'Thank you, Charlie,' she whispered the name softly and the wind whistled around her slightly, making her smile before she stepped back into the warm house to tuck in her daughter for the night.

And in the sky, a single star began to shine, brighter than any other star seen on that night.

Perfection

By Sinéad McHugh, age 16.

The first thing you reach for

The last thing you put down before you go to bed, always

A thought in the back of your head

Constant notifications

Procrastinations between conversations

Always in your hand

Your personal newsstand

Keeping you up to date

With the state

Of society

Reminding you of propriety

Urging you to always look your best

Seems the world is appearance-obsessed

People's lives can look like a dream

But things aren't always what they seem

You won't see the original photo

The tweaking it had to undergo

Hair all done

Makeup to stun

All for a like or two

Any less than a few

Take it down

With a frown

As your confidence bursts like a bubble

Falls to the ground into a pile of rubble

Try again later

Make this one greater

Airbrushed face

Not a thing out of place

Choose the photo with intense selection

This constant pressure for contrived perfection

The Lumberjack's Son

By Maxim Mulligan, age 16.

It was a bright sunny day. Henry was sitting in his garden with his wife and daughter, Lucy and Jane. The day was almost over, but it had been amazing so far. Their garden was a nice, small area surrounded by a hedge wall. It had patterns cut out in the trimmed grass, spirals, wavy lines. There were two stone benches in the corners with tall bushes between and beside them. The hedge wall was neatly trimmed as if it were a painting. He looked to where Lucy sat playing with young Jane. Lucy had long black hair with sky blue eyes. Jane was the younger copy of her mother at the age of nine.

Lucy was from a well-off family who earned their fortune working in the mines. Sadly, they died in a mining accident. Henry was born and raised in the countryside. He lived with his father, a lumberjack, who would return home smelling of the different kinds of trees he worked on from oak and sycamore to spruce and pine. He didn't know his mother as she had died in childbirth and had only been told stories of her.

He smiled to Lucy and Jane and was filled with happiness when Lucy smiled her warm, soft smile back. For a moment, Henry could hear nothing. The birds weren't chirping and singing. The leaves weren't rustling. He looked around, but didn't see anything unusual. His gaze returned to Lucy, but could straight away see something wasn't right. Her gaze seemed cold and distant. She wasn't moving and neither was Jane. He continued to look and try and figure out what was wrong, but to his horror and dismay a crimson stream gently flowed down their necks. The stream became a river and then they fell to the ground. Henry rushed to them to help, but by the time he arrived they were stone dead. Two sharp, dark green, pines lay embedded into the ground with a dark red tip. There lay the two people closest to him in his life taken from him in a matter of seconds. He hugged the limp corpses of his wife and daughter, hoping that this was just a dream that he would awaken from any minute.

Friends and family attended the funeral in the local church. Henry was beyond crying at that point. His eyes were bloodshot both from the crying days before and the lack of sleep. He had come to the funeral in formal attire and tried to clean up his face best he could. The funeral was short and afterwards people came and said a few words to him about how they were sorry for his loss. The graves were small and simple, just like the lives they had lived.

A few days after the funeral, Henry decided to take a walk through the park in the centre of the town. He had stayed in his house for far too long, secluded from the outside world. Too sad to go out or eat. He knew that eventually he would have to go out, to eat, to get on with his life. They would have wanted him to go on with his life if not for himself, for them. As he strolled through the park, he saw young boys and girls running about with their parents. The colourful scenery contrasting with his sad, grey, dark mood. Around corners he would see the occasional gardener picking weeds or watering the flowers.

He continued on through the park, but a strange voice almost like Lucy's floated into his ears. It was faint and murmuring something like

'Come and find me...'

Thinking this was just what his brain wanted him to hear, he ignored it and continued. He thought he was losing it.

'Must be a side effect to them dying,' he'd tell himself. 'Just keep going,' he said.

Some of the other people there looked at him with a confused look. The children who heard him rushed towards their parents and held them close. In the end, he decided to follow the voice. He went just to convince himself that this was just his imagination, but he also went to see Lucy's blue eyes and soft smile once more, if only once.

And so, he followed the voice to the outskirts of the town not too far from his late parents' house. From there he was led down a barely visible path. It went deep into a forest where the light of day burst through a canopy of leaves. Along the floor the trodden path led to what almost looked like a door. Leaves hung down from low lying branches and along vines of light and dark green. He pushed them aside and peered into the space ahead. It was a circle of trees connected by their leaves. It was magical and mysterious to Henry. In the centre, surrounded by a carpet of leaves, was a thick wide stump. Piercing the very centre of the stump was an axe. The handle was made of a dark metal surrounded by a band of leather. The blade glowed in the eerie glow of the light piercing through the leaves. It had a red trim of metal around the top. Henry walked closer and placed both of his hands on the hilt. With a great tug, he dislodged the axe. For a moment, the world seemed to freeze. Not a sound was heard. The wind didn't howl or even whistle. The leaves were still. What broke the silence was what Henry least expected. The axe spoke.

'Hello, Henry,' it said.

Henry was both startled and amazed.

'Lucy!' He exclaimed. 'How?'

'I'll explain later.' She said and then in a more serious tone. 'But now you are in danger.'

'Ha, ha, ha' came a cackling voice from deep within the forest. 'I killed those closest to you. I will show you just how much pain and suffering your father did to me and my brethren.'

Henry could hear leaves rustling to his left. Suddenly a tree burst out of the forest. It had two legs and arms. Its body was covered in pine needles. The sun was setting and darkness had fallen. Before Henry could react, a pine needle shot at him from behind, grazing the top of his shoulder. Blood started to ooze from the wound causing Henry to stagger. Once he regained his balance, he began to run out of the forest, but his exit was blocked by the very same tree. It swung one of its giant arms at him. Henry jumped to the side to dodge. He then swung Lucy at the arm. The axe blade sunk deep into the bark of the tree.

'Arghh!' it yelled in a cry of pain.

Henry seeing his opportunity, ran between the tree's legs. It tried to slash at him again, but just barely missed.

'He can't leave the forest!' Lucy yelled to Henry as they ran.

They almost made it before the tree could recover. But it did and it ran straight towards Henry. Henry dived out of the forest followed by the tree.

It was, however, much less successful. It charged at him and when it got close enough, it tried to slash at him. The tips of its fingers cut through the fabric of Henry's shirt. It left small cuts in Henry's skin, but he was too afraid to notice. The tree's hand, however, seemed to burn when it reached out of the forest boundary. It walked back into the forest and soon faded among the other trees. Henry began to walk back to the town, but Lucy convinced him otherwise, telling him no one would believe him. They decided to go to his parents' house as it was secluded from other people.

'Your life is going to get much tougher now, but I will be with you all the way,' Lucy told him as they walked towards the house.

The cabin was old, bare apart from some old furniture. Henry's head was filled with old memories from his childhood like the time when he cut down a small tree just bigger than his father. There was a staircase to the basement with the same old creaky stairs. The basement was filled with some wood carvings and wood logs in the corner. The small garden outside had long lost its colourful flowers and was filled with dead bushes and weeds. The sun was just beginning to peek out over the horizon but Henry hadn't slept at all over the last day and so went straight to the straw bed at the back wall where his father had slept so long ago.

Henry didn't know what happened to his father. That day started just like any other day. His father went out to chop down some trees and Henry stayed at home carving out one of his first carvings, a beaver. He was only thirteen at the time of the tragedy. He was excited to show his father the final result of his beaver, but his father never came home that day. The people in the nearest village told him that his father must have got lost or some wild beast attacked him. Now Henry knew very clearly what had happened and vowed to get vengeance for his father, Lucy and Jane.

Nightmares plagued him that night. In the nightmare, there was a ghost. It was like a round ball with a flat bottom and short tentacles. It attacked him and when he tried to fight it, it just disappeared and then reappeared in a new place. When he told Lucy about it, she told him the ghost was just plaguing his mind, but he wasn't convinced. There was no food in the house so Henry went into the market and bought some food. He had taken the same path as he did when he went to sell the wood products in the market with his father all those years ago. Most of the food he bought which he had as a child enjoyed, seemed almost tasteless and secretly he went down into the basement and took a good chunk of wood and ate it. He didn't tell Lucy about this, but he continued his strange habit.

Days passed, the dreams stopped occurring, he continued eating wood, but now more frequently. He still didn't tell Lucy about this. Over time his skin had become more orange and had grown fur. One night he had one of by far his strangest dreams. He was walking through the same forest where he found Lucy. This time it was different, instead of the tree that attacked him, a giant beaver attacked him. As the beaver jumped at him, he woke abruptly. There was a shadow on the wall much like the creature from his first dream. He grabbed Lucy and held her in front of him.

'There is nothing there,' she said, 'Calm down.'

He ran towards the kitchen to try and set the ghost on fire with some of the firewood he kept out of the basement. He was flung into a wall by what looked to him like a giant hand. He struck the ground with Lucy causing it to disappear, but then reappeared just like in the dream. By this stage the ghost had made its way to the door of the kitchen so Henry gave up trying to get there. He ran towards the basement to grab a stick to set fire to instead. He ran back up, ducking and weaving around the ghost's arms. He lit the stick and swung it at the ghost. Henry struck the makeshift torch against the wooden walls in an attempt to destroy the ghost that plagued his mind. Finally, the torch found its target and the ghost vanished for good. By this stage the house was on fire, the pictures fell to the ground, shattering the glass. He was about to leave the house when suddenly the remaining flesh on his body began to turn to an orange fur coat. His face turned into that of a beaver and he grew a tail.

'You've been eating wood!' she exclaimed, 'you should have told me.'

But her husband couldn't talk anymore. He ran out of the house to find a group of men from a nearby village had come to see what had started the fire. Upon seeing them, Henry began running to the forest, away from the crowd. There was a clearing which seemed odd. He ran out to hear the men at the house scream in pain and then stop. After the brief moment of silence followed a familiar voice

'Did you really think you could escape me forever? I will show you how wrong you were!' cried the tree that attacked him before.

It charged towards him. This time Henry wasn't running away, but rather towards him. Where the tree's hand that got burnt off before, was now a long, sharp branch that could probably pierce the thickest metal. The tree swung that branch at him, which he dodged and then countered by striking Lucy into the tree's left arm. The axe left a mark from which tree sap flowed. The tree, in a howl of rage stomped a giant foot into the ground. A second later, roots came out of the ground striking Henry's right arm in which he held Lucy. Henry dropped Lucy and sunk his teeth into the tree's chest. It staggered back giving Henry a moment to go on the offensive. Henry bit away more and more bark off of the tree. It swung the spear arm at him sending Henry hurtling into a nearby tree. Henry rose to his feet and bit onto the second attacking arm of the tree. It tried to shake him off but Henry didn't let go and ripped off the arm. The tree let out a howl of pain. Henry continued chewing through the chest of the tree. Henry could tell it was dying but didn't stop. He wanted to make it pay for all it had done. The tree made a final attack skewering Henry through. For a moment, nothing happened until they both fell and Henry transformed back into a human. In his final moments, he looked around but couldn't see the tree or even any footprints. He looked down into his hand and saw a sharp branch covered in blood. He turned to where Lucy lay and whispered his final words

'I'll see you on the other side.'

But the axe gave no response.

Olympus

By Siobhán Walsh, age 17.

You are the daughter of goddesses and queens.

Your blood is nectar,

Your tears are stars.

You are strong.

You are Athena.

Wars and wisdom and weapons and words.

You fight for justice, for yourself and for others.

You are a fighter.

You are Aphrodite.

Love and beauty and smiles and lipstick.

You've seen the bad in the world, but you choose love anyway.

You are a lover.

You are Artemis.

Moonlight and forests and wolves and knives.

You live among the stars and race the moon to bed.

You are a dreamer.

You are Demeter

Nature and nurture and green and life.

You take care of those who need it,

-- and sometimes that means you.

You are a giver.

You are Persephone.
Darkness and flames and flowers and light.
You crowned yourself the queen of hell,
but built your throne from flowers.
You are a miracle.

You are Hestia.
Fire and warmth and home.
You do not deserve to be forgotten.
You are a wonder.

You are Hera.
Strength and power and love and jealousy.
You know your own worth.
You are a woman.
And you are strong.

As You Were

By Catherine Jordan, age 17.

The shop leant to one side. It creaked in the wind, as if at any second it would collapse into debris and dust. The glass front gleamed and the doorway loomed, like the maw of some alien beast. A creature of wood and cement, alien and empty. The neon light of the signs flickered on and off. The heartbeat of a slumbering beast.

A whistling sound – the entire street seemed to prick up an ear, listening. It was as if the bunting stretched across the shopping district decided to stop flapping in the wind. A figure was pounding the beat, her heavy-duty combat boots splattered with mud – the result of running through a paddy field at six o'clock in the morning last week.

She had bright red hair – not the natural shade, but instead the sort that was the colour of apples and twice as shiny – which hung limply around her face, as if it had been severely mistreated. She had a heavy-set face with a cheerful grin, an expression that meant a good-natured sort of trouble, but trouble nonetheless. An ancient leather jacket seemed to hang on her, weighed down by hundreds of trinkets and badges sewn onto the leather. A soft drink bottle top had been glued on beside a pin proclaiming the owner had been to the Taj Mahal. A Spanish anti-fascist badge sat proudly beside a sticker of a cat in a teacup.

She stepped up to the front of the shop. Peered up at the sign above the doorway.

'Glamour and Beauty,' she read off the sign. 'I need some of that, huh?'

Her companion, who had been skulking behind her for the entire journey there, shuffled nervously. He had a five o'clock shadow and deep bags under his eyes; he kept wringing his hands like he was at a funeral. His name was Christopher. He was having a bad week.

'Um. I'm not sure. Uh.' He said. The woman laughed, slapping him on the back. He crumpled like the last leaf of autumn. They watched the shop carefully.

'You're sure they're in there?' The woman said. Shuffling about, she pulled out a pipe. She didn't light it, she just chewed on the end. It looked like it had been chewed a lot.

'Y-yeah. It's been causing so much trouble, you wouldn't believe it. I had to close last Monday, it's been terrible for business. Can you please get it out?' Christopher said.

'Yeah, I'll get them. Gimme a mo'.' The woman glanced at her watch. Two in the morning. Close enough to the witching hour for them to manifest, but late enough so that they'd be tired and withdrawn. Perfect.

The woman stepped into the shop – and then the cheerful expression was gone. She straightened up, and suddenly she was Astrid; bane of poltergeists, remover of spirits, ghost hunter extraordinaire. She took in the interior of the shop.

Clothes lay strewn across every available surface, all tatters and shreds. Glass crunched under her feet. The lightbulbs had been blown out, leaving the shop in deep, dark shadows. Nothing moved. Nothing living, at least. Mirrors for staring at oneself in clothes that wouldn't fit outside the shop had been cracked and destroyed. The cash register had been ripped into shards of metal, and now they lay, glinting, on the floor.

Astrid took it in with an expression of someone with experience. She stepped forwards, mindful of any debris.

'Hello?' She called. 'I'm not here to hurt you. I'm here to help.'

A rustling of fabric on the other side of the shop. Astrid's ears perked up like a cat hearing the can opener. She kept moving, always in that clear, close gait that made it easy to plan the next move. Astrid stepped over a fallen mannequin and froze.

Two eyes were peering out from behind a sign proclaiming that a sale was now on. Something clinked, like a golf ball being rolled around a mouth. Astrid held up her hands, all placating.

'Hey-o. I'm Astrid. I think you're in a bit of a pickle. Don't worry, I'm here to—' Astrid said, but then she had to duck behind a pillar as a couch went flying over her head.

The thing in the shop snarled. It was a guttural sound, like breath wheezing through a collapsed windpipe. Astrid stood up and brushed dirt off herself. She eyed up the other occupant of the building.

It was a woman. To be completely precise, it was an ex-woman. She had pulled blankets and fabrics around herself, like a caterpillar in a cocoon. Only a wan face peered out from the blankets, two dark shadows under her eyes. She was slightly translucent, like someone had sucked the life out of her.

'Hey. Hey. I'm not going to hurt you. You're scared. You were – you just woke up like this, didn't you? With … you were alive, and now you're not.' Astrid said.

The woman didn't speak. Astrid frowned. Normally, ghosts had a purpose. Something they had to do, something they had forgotten or couldn't do during their lives. This one wasn't doing anything. She was just lurking in the dark. Even the blankets made no sense.

Then Astrid noticed the pattern on the fabric and her stomach turned to ice.

'Oh. Oh my God. I'm – I'm sorry.' Astrid rasped. She forgot about safety, she forgot about Christopher outside. She moved towards the woman and sat down beside her.

The woman adjusted her blankets – all of them blue. On one of them, a pattern of little ducks. A pattern of bouncing balls, of soothers. Of storks carrying little bundles. The woman blinked up at Astrid, and her eyes were glass marbles, with deep vicious sorrow in them.

'I'm, I'm sorry,' Astrid said again. The woman moved her blankets again – revealing a small shape wrapped in cloth, and clutched to her thin chest. The ghost had the way that the stomach skin stretched after pregnancy, all tired skin pulled too taut. The bundle lay, unmoving. Cold. Dead. 'I really am.'

The ghost's neck was bruised. Her windpipe had collapsed. She breathed – she didn't need to now, it was just a habit that she'd soon grow out of – in short sharp bursts, her dead lungs wheezing.

'People, people can be cruel,' Astrid whispered, barely above a breath. 'But, but that's over. You don't have to stay here any longer.'

The woman rummaged around her neck, pulled out a string of beads made of wood and clay. They were worn, well-thumbed and used. The woman looked questioning up at Astrid. She frowned, looking down at the ghost.

'I … I'm not sure. Maybe. Maybe it's that heaven. But it'll be better than here.' Astrid said.

The woman sighed, a long sound that felt like nails and screws on her throat. She said nothing. Astrid shuffled, not knowing what to do.

'Uh. I have – I have stuff. Usually, we'd sing you to sleep. But I'm not good at that. So, uh.' Astrid pulled out her phone. Clicked onto the video player. They watched an advertisement for sofas, unblinking, and then soft nursery rhymes began to play out of the tinny speaker.

The woman watched the video buffer, the seconds ticking by. When the video ended, Astrid clicked onto the next one. The third, the fourth. When they were on the sixth, the woman turned to her. She rummaged about, then pulled off her rosary. Astrid let her pull on her hand until the ghost gently placed the beads in her palm. Dead, brittle fingers closed her own over it.

'I can't take this. This is, this is yours.' Astrid said.

The woman shook her head, having none of it. Then she reached over and clicked onto the seventh video. They watched until Astrid's mobile data ran out, then they replaced the others until the battery was gone. As the videos clicked by, the woman rocked the little bundle back and forth, to the tune of the lullabies.

The screen faded to black, power gone. Astrid risked a look at the ghost. She was asleep, her sorrowful features calm in rest. The bundle was back on her chest, close to her unbeating heart. Her breathing was even again.

'Good night.' Astrid whispered. And then she left, not waiting to see the figure crouched between the stands and mannequins disappear like snow in the sun. They all went like that, eventually. Off to whatever came next. Leaving nothing behind but a trinket or a memory.

She didn't think much as she walked by Christopher, ignoring his complaints about business. She brushed off his yammerings and cursing of ghost. It was as if her head was empty, white noise in the place of thoughts. She got into her car – plugged in her phone. A spool of thread from the side compartment let Astrid sew the rosary onto her jacket, near a poppet made of dead grass and a twisted paperclip. It lay, gleaming with tears from her own eyes, with messy stitches beside her badges.

Then Astrid sat in her car, in the buzzing silence. She felt empty, all hollowed out. Her phone vibrated to say it was charged again. Her hands trembled, her mind replaying the events in the shop.

She listened to those nursery rhymes all the way home.

May

By Hollie Hannon, age 17.

They told me love was

A bouquet of red roses

A diamond ring and

Promises that would last forever

'Love is hard to find,' they told us

'You might spend your whole life searching for it.'

And I believed them.

But you showed me love could be

A purple sky in winter,

Your flower garden that bloomed all the colours of your heart

And your wooden cuckoo clock that you kept polished

In the living room.

Simple things like your voice I remember so well

'How are you, precious,' you told me everyday

Swinging me onto the safehold of your lap

And I remember

You reading me stories,

Stories of old that you made feel timeless.

I remember your eyes skimming over the black and white pages that you instantly

Turned to the shades of the rainbow

I remember walking back from the bog with you

My clothes and face streaked with mud that felt like a favourite shade of paint

Pulling up new potatoes in your vegetable patch

And breathing life into them.

I remember sitting on your shoulders watching the horses graze in the field

Where they would come running to the rattle, like dice, of seven sugar cubes,

But most of all I remember your smile

A smile that I knew so well

And would keep stored in my head forever

Love was made of you,

And it broke me

When you passed on at 9.15 in your hospital room.

I can only love you now from a distance

A love so strong and painful it split me

And my world in half,

But even though it hurts

And bears a cross I was never ready to carry

It's better than having never felt it at all.